W9-ASL-852

THE DREADED CLIFF

hjbfi   HEB
NICHO

DISCARD

Nichols, Terry, author
The dreaded cliff
33410017032774   03-10-2021

Hebron Public Library
201 W. Sigler Street
Hebron, IN 46341

ISBN: 9781951122126 (paperback)/9781951122171 (ebook)
LCCN: 2020939370
Copyright © 2020 by Terry Nichols
Cover illustration © 2020 by Odessa Sawyer
Cover design: Geoff Habiger
Interior illustrations © 2020 by Odessa Sawyer

Printed in the United States of America.

Names, characters, and incidents depicted in this book are products of the author's imagination or are used fictitiously. Any resemblance to actual events, locales, organizations, or persons, living or dead, is entirely coincidental and beyond the intent of the author or the publisher.

All rights reserved. No part of this book may be reproduced or transmitted in any form or by any means, electronic or mechanical, including photocopying, recording or by any information storage or retrieval system without written permission of the publisher, except for the inclusion of brief quotations in a review.
Kinkajou Press
9 Mockingbird Hill Rd
Tijeras, New Mexico 87059
info@kinkajoupress.com
www.kinkajoupress.com

THE DREADED CLIFF

By

Terry Nichols

Illustrated by

Odessa Sawyer

Kinkajou Press

For Cyrus and Dylan

Table of Contents

CHAPTER ONE
REMEMBER THE CLIFF

"I'm a *goddess*." Flora loved saying those words. Even when no one was around. When she was happy and well-fed the words just flowed, and they pleased her. It felt much better than saying, "I'm a chunky packrat."

She was a goddess, for sure. A *packrat* goddess.

As packrats go, Flora *was* rather chunky, even juicy—like the prickly pear cactus pads she adored eating. But she hardly ever thought about her chunkiness.

Mostly she thought about food: hunting it, sniffing it, chomping it. Especially prickly pear cactus pads. She bit them and squished, spurting glorious slime from her mouth. That's when life was perfect for Flora.

But perfect never lasts. Even for a packrat goddess.

#

"Oh, I can't wait, I *can't wait!*" The scent made her toes and teeth itch for a munch. "But wait..." Flora glanced skyward. Was she safe? For now. Probably.

Her goddess folds jiggled as she scooted from the juniper tree to her favorite food.

Chomp, slobber-slobber. She gnawed around the clusters of spines, slurping the gooey juices. "Oh yum, oh yum."

Then in mid-munch Flora froze and sniffed the air. A shadow lurked behind a crooked chain of cactus pads. The breeze shifted, and Flora let out a sigh of relief when she smelled her cousin.

"Gertrude!" Flora's twirled her whiskers.

"Flora! You gave me a fright!" Gertrude toddled from her hiding place. "What are you doing out this late? It's nearly dawn."

"I want to snibble a snack before heading home."

"Huh? What are you talking about?" Gertrude puckered her nose. "You're always saying crazy words that don't make sense."

"Wait, maybe that's not right…" Flora's mouth oozed cactus snot, which helped her sort through the clutter of words in her head. "Hmm, snibble—snubble—snobble—nobble—nibble. Oh, I meant *nibble*. But I like 'snibble' better. I want to snibble a snack before—"

"*Hraaaaahh!*" Gertrude bellowed a yawn, plugging Flora's spout of words and catching her attention. Something seemed wrong with Gertrude. She looked worn-out and plump-less. Her shiny fur had dulled, and her eyes were sunken and crinkly around the edges.

"Gertrude, are you alright? Is it your babies?"

She nodded. "My pups are *sooo* hungry. They clamp on and suckle nonstop. I have to drag them around with me. Except for tonight when they all fell asleep and lost their grip and I could get away." Her voice turned to a whisper. "They're adorable, Flora, but I'm afraid I can't do this much longer."

"Eat a healthy cactus pad so you can stay strong." Flora tightened her mouth. Her best friend might not survive the food demands of her babies. Flora hadn't yet raised pups of her own, she knew that motherhood for a packrat was a busy time. And dangerous for her health.

"Thanks, but I need to get back. I'm sure they're hungry again. They shouldn't leave the safety of the nest to look for me."

Gertrude twitched her nose; Flora's stomach tightened. Before Gertrude scuttled off to the woodpile, Flora expected *the warning* from Gertrude. THE WARNING. The strange, bothersome warning. It always tied her gut in knots. That dreadful warning would soon hit her ears. She wished she didn't have to hear it.

"Remember the cliff, Flora. Beware of the dreaded cliff."

Gertrude's deadly serious voice shook a little from her fear of the cliff. Every packrat knew there was something awful about that place. But Flora didn't want to think about it.

Forgetting the cactus spines she had clipped earlier, she headed for her nest in the jangly-crate—a big metal box that seemed to float in the air on round black legs.

Beyond the jangly-crate past the cottonwood trees loomed a rising sandstone wall. Boulders on the ground guarded a crack slashing the face of the wall. A thorny tangle of sticks crammed that dark opening, telling all to stay away.

The dreaded cliff. Ever since Flora was a wee

hairless pup, her mother had cautioned her with the same words used by Gertrude: Remember. Beware.

By the time she was under the jangly-crate, her insides were all twisted. She needed comfort, relief. Flora hopped onto the metal attached to the underside of the jangly-crate where she had stashed her nest.

A blanket of treasures, glued together with her urine, wrapped around her. Bark shreds, cactus spines, crusty animal droppings, piñon pine cones, flattened bits of metal with rippled edges, twirly metal spikes, curls of twisted metal, and smooth glassy balls were all there, just as she liked. Snuggling deeper, she closed her eyes.

Her knotted stomach took a long time to loosen and let go of Gertrude's warning. But like a sticky black shadow, her mother's words stayed, gripping every crinkle of her body.

Remember. Beware.

CHAPTER TWO
PACKRAT ETIQUETTE

The next night as stars speckled the inky sky, Flora pranced and snuffled along sandy paths, hoping to discover a delicacy to thrill her picky taste buds.

She sniffed at the munch mound where she and Gertrude had spent many happy hours looking for tasty scraps. "The smell of that warty rind is gruesome. But this crispy glob is tempting my tongue." A food critic of sorts, Flora could not resist commenting.

On this particular night, however, Flora felt

pulled from the munch mound to the other side of the bloated burrow—a huge chamber of sharp corners and towering sides, the home of the giant two-legged rodents. "Strange creatures." Flora crept along the stiff wall muttering. "The big rodents must be sizzly-hot, so they can heat their gigantic burrow in cold times."

Her legs shook a little. "Oh my, the dreaded cliff, behind those trees. I won't look." The place was creepy. She didn't look, but she could feel that rock face. Immense. Reaching through the trees, pushing on her. Why was she even there? She wasn't sure. An invisible lasso had captured Flora's senses and tugged her along.

Above, a wooden surface jutted out from the bloated burrow. No place for a packrat. But her nose itched, especially when she saw the steps. She felt a mighty urge to scamper away, but Flora climbed, peered around, and climbed again.

At the top her nose didn't just itch, it *throbbed* and her stomach roared. Fat rounded vegetables glistened on plants growing in a box packed with dirt. The promise of a taste delight pulled her like a warm juicy animal lures a hungry mosquito. She sniffed a purple blob and nibbled.

No words, no words—at first there were *no* words to describe the flavor. Until she chewed and swished her tongue around the mouthful several times. Her special word moment had arrived. That word was only for food way better than delicious, far beyond yummy, the tastiest of tasty. Top gourmet. Only when she entered food heaven did she use her special word.

Quickly she murmured it, so she wouldn't interrupt her eating.

"*Sublime.*"

Her eyes grew dreamy as she whittled the blob to its stem.

With her belly puffed and happy, Flora nipped some leaves, stuffed them in her mouth, and scampered down the steps—hardly noticing the dreaded cliff.

"Such a heavenly food. Pure sublimation." The first taste lingered on her tongue. "Wait, that's not right. I meant to say, 'pure subliming.' Or maybe I should have said, '*sublime.*'"

Sometimes she got mixed-up when she used words, mostly the special words. No matter. She yippee-hopped as she turned the corner of the bloated burrow, nearly crashing into Gertrude, cactus spines cramming her mouth. She was also dragging her three squirmy pups, latched to her nipples like hairy monster leeches, suckling away.

"It was super amazing, Gertrude—I found

food heaven. You *must* taste it."

"On the flat place high on the bloated burrow? In full view of the...dreaded cliff? Oh, no, never... it's much too dangerous."

Flora ignored Gertrude's caution. After all, one trip to food heaven was never enough. The next night she climbed the steps again. The bigness of the dreaded cliff pressed the air on her back, but she tried to ignore it.

When she reached the top, she sensed danger—the kind that makes a packrat heart beat double-time.

Another packrat—jumbo-size, a hefty boy requiring great caution. Perched on the box, his paws hugged a gleaming vegetable. Over the box edge spilled his hairy tail.

Flora drooled, shifted, and watched him eat the feast—*her* feast, her ticket to food heaven. Her heart pounded and voices argued in her head.

Scram Flora.

No, wait. He should go.

Fight maybe.

What? Fraidy-Flora never fights—especially a jumbo-size packrat!

But...but...food heaven...

Arguing with herself in her head was nothing new. Especially when she was hungry or nervous.

She was both at the moment.

After a packrat eternity, Flora's empty stomach screamed.

Gathering her wits, she found the right word: *clever*. She needed to be clever. And sometimes being clever meant acting in a way totally opposite to what she first felt like doing. In this case clever meant using manners. Good manners. Her mother called it "packrat etiquette."

"Hello there," she squeaked in a shaky voice. "I'm hungry." But the packrat kept eating. Maybe she wasn't using the etiquette right.

Flora moved closer to the box. The jumbo-size packrat was scraping the last bits of a shiny blob, now chewed to a nubbin. Flakes of purple skin littered the area.

"I said hello," Flora shouted. Surely that was better etiquette.

The packrat stopped eating, twisted his head, and eyeballed Flora. He shuffled off the box and landed, thudding like a gob of hairy mashed potatoes.

Flora sat glued to the flat surface below her. Her thin ribs tightened. *The etiquette*, she scolded herself, *the etiquette wasn't right.*

Grunting with each step, he creaked to within whiskers of Flora and sniffy-sniff-sniffed. His frightful bulk, no doubt huge from a regular diet of purple blobs, towered over the trembling Flora.

CHAPTER THREE
BIGGER THAN LIFE

"Oh, hello dearie, I didn't see you there. My eyes aren't what they used to be." The grandmotherly voice washed Flora in relief.

Such an enormous packrat. Was that a double chin? Fat rolls circling her *tail*? And so old. Like bald-spots-tattered-ears-snaggletooth old. She lugged along on stiff legs, puffing and pausing with every move.

"Excuse me, but I am so very hungry, and these blobs are so very subliminal...I mean sublime. May I eat some?"

"Help yourself. I shouldn't eat these eggplants anyway. Gives me gas."

Flora wasted no time gorging on an eggplant-blob. She snipped purple blossoms for decorating her nest, stuffed them in her mouth, and hopped from the box.

"Thank you for sharing. I feel sublimated." Bits of delicate petals flew from her mouth. The "sublimated" word didn't sound right, but the packrat etiquette felt perfect. "I must be going now."

"Hold on there, dearie. What's your hurry? Stay and chat with me." Her bulging eyes, clouded with age, smiled at Flora.

Wait, wait. Flora *never* chitchatted with a stranger. No telling what the stranger might say, or do, or want. Even if the stranger only wanted to chat about the breeze or the moon or other small things, still Flora would have to think of something to say and try to sound clever. And try not to offend her. It was much safer to keep to herself, hunt for food with Gertrude sometimes, and snuggle in her perfect cozy nest.

But something was calming about the old packrat's voice and crinkled eyes. Despite her fears, Flora settled next to the old one.

A glowing ball of moon softened the night, touching mounds of sagebrush and brushing sandstone boulders. Cottonwood trees cast deep shadows. Threads of light traveled through the leafy branches and played with chirping crickets and creatures scuttling through dried leaves.

For a moment Flora's eyes fell on the jagged crack in the dreaded cliff. She looked away.

"What's the trouble, dearie? Isn't this a beautiful night? It's bright enough for discovering all kinds of things, things you've never imagined."

"It *is* bright out." Flora felt bold with the kindly stranger. "But the dreaded cliff—it frightens me." Even though she tried not to look, her eyes seemed captured like a bug in a spider's web.

"The cliff? Why, that holds our special place, dearie." The old packrat paused. "What is your name?" She turned toward Flora, straining to hear.

"My name is Flora."

The scraggly grey whiskers twitched. "Hmm, Flora." Eyes half-closed, she cocked her head. Her wrinkly face brightened. "Oh yes, Flora. I'm Grandma Mimi, your mother's great-grandmother. You're the one who amazed your mother when you talked long before your brother and sister." The old packrat chuckled.

Warmth flooded Flora's body. Warmth and memory. Her mother had spoken many times of this very grandmother, always with great respect.

"Oh my, Grandma Mimi. My mother said you raised litter after litter of pups for as long as she could remember. I thought you were gone."

All packrats knew about the old one. Not only had she lived a long time, but she was also wise and knew the best answers to many questions. Even questions a packrat would never think to ask. At least that's what Flora had heard from her mother. Grandma Mimi was an empress, a hero, a packrat idol so to speak. Now here she was sitting next to Flora, bigger than life.

CHAPTER FOUR
SPARKLY TREASURE

They had never before met. But as they shared that night, bellies tight with eggplant and starry air brushing their fur, the two packrats talked as the long-lost family they were.

Flora prattled nonstop, starting with her munch mound searches with Gertrude. "Sometimes the tidbits are super delicious. Mostly it's a mash-mish, a stew of gustatory delight."

"Uh-huh, mash-mish." Grandma Mimi nodded.

"The word 'gustatory' is all about the taste of food, Grandma Mimi."

"Hmm, gustatory." The corners of Grandma Mimi's mouth rose.

"But sometimes the munch mound gets hot and steamy, and everything is disgusting, and we're lucky if we find anything tasty.

"And I found the perfect place for my nest— the bottom of the jangly-crate. It's a big box-like thing that clangs and pings when it rains and makes ding-y noises when the air heats up or cools down."

"Clangs and pings? Strange—"

"It's so strange—the jangly-crate is up in the air and round black legs attach it to the ground. They stink when the air is hot." Flora panted as she chattered.

"And sometimes I find shiny and precious things in the grass nearby. They lavish-ish beauty in my nest." Adding the extra "ish" to the "lavish" word felt so satisfying.

Grandma Mimi's eyes drooped to narrow slits.

"That's where I found slick balls that flash colors, and tiny stiff animals, and skinny discs that sparkle. Those things grow in that place, or maybe the rain brings them, I'm not sure, but I look every night and presto, I find them—like magic. Oh yes, and by the berry plants, I found the crazy quilt. It's a strange piece of furless fur, and it's springy soft in my nest.

"But, Grandma Mimi, tell me about your life." Asking about the old one was surely good pack-rat etiquette. Besides by now, Flora was a little breathless.

Grandma Mimi widened her eyes and shook her whiskers. "Oh, young one, I've seen the seasons change many times. I've raised lots of pups, and I don't know how many grandpups and great-grandpups and great-great-grandpups I have. The cold times seem even colder, and I can't hear or see so well anymore. But I sure do love these eggplants."

They both grew quiet. Flora felt safe sitting next to this living legend, who seemed so calm, so confident.

Grandma Mimi gazed at the dreaded cliff. "I miss our special place. I miss our true home." There was a longing, a deep sadness in her quivering voice, unlike her earlier peaceful mood.

"Grandma Mimi, what are you saying? What home? The...the dreaded cliff?"

"Flora, there are reasons why packrats call it dreaded. But first, we try to *remember* the cliff. We packrats remember it because it's the place where we began."

Flora's stomach churned. But Grandma Mimi's

soft voice calmed her.

"Look closely, Flora, at the crack in the cliff."

Feeling stronger with Grandma Mimi's presence, Flora for the first time ever looked fully at the dark scab on the cliff. As she stared into that moonlit space, her eyes widened. The fur on her back stood on end and her whiskers trembled.

The clump of sticks plugging that void looked like the sticks she had crammed in the narrow space protecting her own nest. The secret in the crack shimmered.

"It's a packrat home," whispered Flora.

"That's right, Flora. It's our ancestral home—the great packrat birthplace. Our packrat ancestors—mothers and grandmothers, our family who came before us—raised their young there."

"Our family? Ancestors from long ago?" This was a lot to take in. She barely remembered her most recent family. Her mother she'd not seen since leaving the nest. A brother and sister had struck out on their own as she had and were no longer in her life. And she never knew her father, because packrat fathers never stick around. An empty spot in her heart spoke the lonely truth: her only family was Cousin Gertrude, whom she had found right after she left the nest.

But not anymore. Now her family included

Grandma Mimi. And, from what she was saying, all those packrats who had lived in the ancestral packrat home in the crack were family, too. Even though they were from long ago.

"This is unreal. The old packrat home is amazing!" Flora stretched her paws, allowing a growing warmth to fill them.

"It's more than amazing, Flora." Grandma Mimi's voice grew strong. "It is the place that makes us who we are."

Her words were alive, breathing and pulsing. *It is the place that makes us who we are.* What did that mean? Flora scrunched her face, trying to sort her thoughts.

Somehow that place was important to packrats being packrats. How could the packrat birthplace make her more of a packrat? Flora already felt pretty packrat-ty, even though she hadn't been born there. Unless, oh no, *unless* she wasn't a real packrat! Maybe she was a fake packrat! Or maybe she'd never be a good enough packrat, or would never grow into an adult packrat, because she hadn't lived in the ancestral packrat home.

"But...I...*feel* like a packrat and I have packrat whiskers, and a packrat hangout with my amazing collection of stuff, and...and...I don't understand!" Flora turned to Grandma Mimi, who looked gently at her.

"For many seasons our ancestors built in the crack. They left thick walls of sticks, bones, spiny cactus pieces, and other precious objects. On each piece, the packrats left their pawprints and tooth-marks."

"If I could get closer, I could touch those walls and see those treasures and their marks, couldn't I, Grandma Mimi?"

"You could, Flora. And our packrat ancestors left something else."

"That's a lot already. What else did they leave?"

"Memories of their lives—the joys of birthing, feeding, and raising their young there."

"They could do that? Leave their memories?"

"Yes, Flora, in the walls, in that place."

Whoa! Flora had to think extra hard about that. "Since there were so many packrats, there must be a lot of happy memories in those walls."

"And sad memories, too." Grandma Mimi peered at Flora and sighed. "But no matter what she left, each packrat mother knew she was for-ever a part of that great packrat birthplace. Each was part of a story much bigger than herself."

Part of a bigger story...Flora's head was stretching, puffing, trying to understand. Memo-ries. Stories. Her own nest was a big story. When she looked at each treasure, she remembered where she found it and how she felt about discovering it. Her nest was full of memories, all making a luscious story about herself that made her feel good. The ancestral home in the cliff told an even bigger story, and all the packrats who had lived there were hooked together inside that story. Forever.

Now she understood why packrats said, "remember the cliff." It had always sounded like a warning, but it wasn't. Instead, it was a message to remind packrats of the cliff's special story—its *packrat* story.

But the next part of the cliff warning still bothered her.

"If it's so important to us, Grandma Mimi, why do packrats call the cliff 'dreaded' and tell others to 'beware'?"

The old packrat lowered her head for a moment. Her eyes grew watery.

"For a long time, packrats safely raised their young there. But one day everything changed. About four summers ago, a litter of pups, almost ready to leave the nest, met a terrible fate." Her voice grew small. "A beast, an awful beast, invaded the packrat home while the mother was gathering food. When she returned, her sweet babies, all of them, were gone." She choked on her last words.

A chill traveled down each of Flora's paws. Her mother had warned her of the predators who would snack on her—coyotes, foxes, hawks, owls, and even the cat. She had seen all of those creatures at least once, and the cat many times. That feline frightened her the most. It skulked under juniper trees, scratched in the dried needle-like leaves, and left foul-smelling droppings. One night she saw a squealing mouse clamped in its mouth. The mouse's ears flapped; the cat's eyes, peering from its black face, glowed sickly green.

The cat could wrap its jaws around a packrat. Even a curvy packrat. Flora avoided that demon.

But none of these creatures, including the cat, could get past the heap of sticks and cactus spines around a packrat nest—especially that fortress, the ancestral packrat home in the crack. Even so, some creature had wiped out an entire packrat litter. Whatever it was, Flora did not want to think about it. Or meet it. Ever.

"Can't we go back?"

"Not as long as he's there. That's why packrats warn each other to stay away. He's claimed our place for himself. He captures packrats and drags them there. Many have become his victims."

Grandma Mimi shriveled.

Flora's insides grew icy. That killer beast was still around. Had he attacked members of *her* family? Since leaving her mother's nest, she had seen only her brother, once, carrying shreds of juniper bark near the graveled path. Where was her sister? And mother? She should have seen them at the munch mound and prickly pear cactus, or in the grove of spikey yuccas where she plucked yucca fruits and blossoms. They all *had* to be safe—her mother had always warned to beware of the dreaded cliff.

The sickness in her stomach turned to an ache, settling in her heart. She ached for Grandma Mimi and all packrats—especially herself. With the awful beast ruling the ancestral home, no packrat could ever return. She would never feel its comfort or add her special cactus pad or sparkly jewel to the walls built by the packrats before her. She would never be a part of its story.

The cliff was a mere scramble away, so clear now, so urgent. In the crack, a crowd of whiskered packrat faces appeared and faded into its shadows, like stars peeking through shifting clouds. Each face held its own special energy now a part of that old home. That dark empty place in Flora's heart fluttered, and she almost called out, "I'm here. You see? I'm here!"

A movement startled her, grabbing her breath. Did something stir in the crack, disturb a stick, rustle in the dry leaves below? Or had she imagined it?

Flora glanced at Grandma Mimi. Her eyes widened, ever so slightly, then narrowed as she focused on the crack. Grandma Mimi had noticed it also.

She sucked in air and spoke quickly. "Flora, thank you for talking with an old packrat. I see you have much to do. I'll just sit here awhile and remember our old home." Flora's whiskers sagged with worry.

"I'm so happy I found you, Grandma Mimi. Thank you for teaching me about the packrat birthplace in the crack. It's a special place. I hope we can talk again soon." Flora felt as if she were making a promise, but she wasn't sure what it was about. All she knew for sure was she craved the comfort of her nest.

Stuffing the eggplant blossoms she'd snipped earlier in her mouth, she plopped down the stairs. Her insides tightened. She expected to hear the warning she always heard after meeting another packrat. Instead, she heard something else: "Flora, look behind the water barrel for the mirror. I think you should have it."

She had no idea what a mirror was. But still, behind the water barrel, she looked. A small pool of solid water—or at least that's what it looked like—glinted. It was slicky-smooth and she sniffed around its sharp edges. The blossoms fell from her jaws. Carefully she clamped her teeth around this treasure and towed it to the jangly-crate.

Flora marveled at how this wondrous thing propped up in her nest reflected the pebbles and twigs and treasures. The slightest bit of light danced on its surface. *Grandma Mimi called it a mirror. It's perfect, just as I like it.*

As she closed her eyes, the shadows stuck to her body from her mother's cliff warnings had grown lighter and less sticky, as though she could lift the corners and peek underneath.

CHAPTER FIVE
TAKEN AWAY

Words filled her dreams and they were doing crazy things. They bashed into each other and split apart and scattered and multiplied like a rattled nest of ants. Usually, Flora loved words—big ones, strange ones, funny ones—but the dream words threw her into a tizzy. The worst part of her dream was she needed to understand them or else she would die.

Flora awoke with a jerk.

"Too light outside. It's not time to rise."

She snapped into her body, into the present.

Her home shook with dreadful noises, coming from its roof right above.

"The two-legged rodents—they're stomping and tromping my home. They're taking over!"

She had lived in her safe perfect nest for many full moons. This had never happened. Although the two-legged pup had romped around the jangly-crate a few times, he had never stayed long, and it wasn't like this. Now the constant racket tossed Flora like a beetle dropped in a gushing stream.

Voices clanged in her head.

Run for it, now!

But it's glaring daylight.

You're not safe here.

I'll just wait. They'll stop soon.

But they'll find you, destroy your nest. They'll destroy you!

She snuggled deeper. Her precious treasures gave little comfort. When the noise faded now and then she dozed, hoping the two-legged rodents would stay away. But they returned.

By evening, her normal time to awaken, the never-ending activity had jarred her into exhaustion. For the last time the two-legged pup's voice rang out as he climbed into the jangly-crate. Blasts of noise shook her home.

And then, a deep rumble—totally foreign to Flora—shook her to the core. Her home lurched, she rolled. The black legs crunched along the gravel pathway. Flora buried her head under her paws and squeezed her eyes shut. She swayed as the jangly-crate rounded a corner onto a smooth surface. The noise screamed; she screamed.

Flora tried to breathe her fright away. But she panted harder, choking and making screechy noises. Her thoughts raced, images tumbled: prickly pear cactus, big juniper tree, eggplant treats, munch mound, packrat birthplace, ancestral home, stolen pups. Evil beast. Remember the cliff. Remember the cliff. *Oh Gertrude, oh Grandma Mimi.*

The growling crate chattered her teeth, her toes, taking her farther, farther away, away from all she knew.

The crack appeared, the dark crack with the old packrat home fixed in its opening. In her head, she saw it framed by light. Her heart reached out to this place, this place she had never known, this place that was home for a string of packrat mothers and grandmothers and great-grandmothers and great-great-grandmothers and on and on and on, all connected to one another, all related by blood and thought and heart and story, through countless moons and seasons and lifetimes upon lifetimes...her heart touched this place, and she felt comforted. Flora floated into a deep sleep as she was taken to the unknown.

CHAPTER SIX
NEW TERRITORY

Flora awoke, breathing heavily in the eerie quiet.

"I'm back. I'm back home on the gravel path near the big juniper tree."

But sharp clanging and the two-legged pup's squealing told her differently. She crinkled her nose. Something sizzled above, creating an odor that spoiled her nest, making her gag.

For a long time, the jangly-crate shook as the two-legged rodents jostled each other and squeaked and roared, banged and clanged, scraped, scratched, and tapped, splashed liquid, bounced and thumped things around, and fought with pieces of the jangly crate itself. The pup seemed to be tapping on something hard, and his voice grew whiny as the night wore on.

Waiting for the racket to calm, Flora was a prisoner in her own nest. But after a while, the thin streams of light reaching her through cracks above grew dark. All was quiet, except for the odd bursts of vibrations that sounded like the buzz of an aging bumblebee.

"Is it over? Oh please, let it be over." Flora listened for a signal telling her it was safe to move.

It finally came—the grumble of her empty stomach.

With whiskers shaking, she moved to the edge of her nest and dropped to the rock-hard ground—unlike the sandy earth in the place she knew well.

Flora crept from beneath the jangly-crate, heart pounding with every step. Beyond, the ground rose and fell in stiff sand dunes, similar to huge scoops of solid mud piled around one another. The jangly-crate sat on the top of the largest scoop of slick rock. At the edges where the rock mounds melted, plants and stones dotted flat pockets of sand.

In one of the sandy spots, Flora spied sagebrush. She scampered down the slope, leaned her front paws on a branch, and plucked small flowers off the upright stems. In another sandy pool, she chewed a prickly pear cactus. After quieting her stomach rumbles, she could analyze her situation.

"How can I still be alive, after all those dreadful noises?" She looked at her tiny pointed claws. "I can see my toes. I'm alive. That's unmistakable."

Her analysis was going well. She scanned around her. "This place seems...different. All this rock! No big juniper tree. Or munch mound...or the bloated burrow of the giant two-legged rodents." Her voice quivered a wee bit. "I don't see Gertrude or Grandma Mimi." As she continued to whisper aloud, she felt stronger. "This is not the place I know. That's indu-bable." That word wasn't right. No matter, Flora was sure she was in new territory.

"No telling how many creatures want to eat me here." She gulped and glanced at the sky.

"I guess it could be worse—I have my nest. I've found food. The two-legged rodents don't even know I'm here. I guess that doesn't matter.

"The two-legged rodents have never moved the jangly-crate. Will they ever go back to their bloated burrow? Such a huge burrow. Maybe it got too cold for them. Or maybe they're here on a mission. Maybe they're teaching their pup how to hunt for food." Flora imagined the spindly two-legged pup, crawling on all fours, chomping a prickly pear pad.

"I need to stay close to my nest. In case the jangly-crate moves. I don't want to lose my nest." Visions of the munch mound, the prickly pear cactus, the eggplants, Grandma Mimi and Gertrude, even the cliff—all pulled on Flora.

"I need to stay alert." She swallowed hard. But didn't say her worst fear: she might never go home.

After speaking her careful analysis Flora felt better. She needed to get back to the jangly-crate at the top of the rocky slope. But what was that big bush? Its narrow stems grew straight up in clusters. No leaves—how strange. A skeleton plant that looked dead.

"Aha! Those twigs are perfect for my nest." She skipped to the bush and snipped with her sharp teeth. Mouth stuffed, she climbed the slope to her nest in the jangly-crate and placed the treasures. But one batch was not enough. Over several hours she traveled back and forth from the bush to her nest, carrying fresh twigs.

The cool night was perfect for her work. But in Flora's careful analysis, she hadn't noticed clouds had blotted out the waning moon.

The air stirred, ruffling her fur and flapping her ears. *Kerplop!* She shook a water droplet off her nose and tugged harder on the stem that would fill the perfect spot in her nest.

An angry flash blinded her; a thunderclap flattened her body. Raindrops pelted her fur until it dripped. She looked for the jangly-crate with her warm nest.

But the jangly-crate had vanished. Sheets of water glistened on the rocky slopes and collected in streams at the bottom. Gooey muck oozed between her padded toes and crept up her tiny paws.

"Oh my." Flora dropped the stems from her mouth and glanced from side to side. "Oh *my!*" Her shout was lost in a roar of pounding water.

CHAPTER SEVEN
ACCIDENTAL GUEST

Puffing hard, Flora pulled each foot from a sucking hole that tried to swallow each trembling leg. But when she stepped from the holes, her feet sank again in the shifting goop. *Slurp-splat! Slurp-splat!* The ground itself was moving under her, and she had to keep slurp-splatting, slurp-splatting until she moved from the pudding sand to solid rock.

Water streamed around her and over her paws.

"My nest, my nest! Run for my nest!" But the

fierce downpour and struggle with the quicksand made her lose all sense of direction. She ran one way, then another, like a fish darting to and fro in a watery world. Moaning and yelping, Flora scampered over a log, slapped onto the rough rock on the other side, and tumbled like a pinecone.

"Yeeoowww!" Flipping, rolling, spinning, flying, she was utterly out of control. Rain bullets pelted, plants snagged, twigs crackled, and the ground pounded. A whir of flailing paws searched for a lifeline to halt her plunge.

Bonk! The trunk of a sagebrush tossed her into the mud. A hole beckoned. Shaking her woozy head, Flora squirmed her beaten body into the opening.

Nosing deeper in the tunnel, she crept into a warm chamber padded with dry grass smelling of some creature's urine. Flora panted while her scattered thoughts settled and her eyes adjusted to the darkness.

"Whoa!" She sucked her breath and drew back. Alien eyes glared.

"*Who* are *you?*"

The voice curled her ample ears. She had intruded into someone's burrow and was nose-to-nose with its owner. Her mouth felt pasted shut, but she had to say something. Anything.

"I'm…I'm Flora. I guess…I *think* I'm out for a walk?" She tried to sound brave, but she could barely hear herself. And she didn't mean to ask a question.

Silence—a long, tense silence.

She tried again, this time gushing. "The storm sent me here, I think, and I can't find my nest, and I don't know where my home is, and I'm so tired, and oh, my head hurts, and I don't know what to do."

The eyes blinked and grew larger. The stranger sniffed, blowing warm puffs all over her face and tickling her muzzle with fine whiskers. She did not dare flinch.

"You know," squeaked a voice right into her ear, "you're in *my* palace." Flora's full-figured body felt extra full right then. She wanted to hightail it out of there, but she was stuck in the tight chamber.

"Behold, King Cyrus," the creature said. Flora's eardrums ached as the whiny voice continued, speaking each work carefully. "*You* know, *Cyrus*—King of the Kangaroo Rats."

In the dim light, she saw a pointy nose raised high. It crowned a sleek body poised on muscular hind legs. His much smaller front paws flapped like an extra set of ears. A thinly haired tail waved a regal tuft of fluff.

A kangaroo rat. Her mother had taught her about this creature, which lives in its underground burrow during the hot day, plugging the openings to keep it humid. A kangaroo rat could eat only dry seeds and never need a drink of water. But packrats needed to eat juicy, fleshy plants for moisture.

She'd learned a lot about kangaroo rats but knew nothing about kangaroo rat *kings*.

Gathering courage, she addressed the royal snout.

"Sir, I mean your grace, er...uh...your highness. I am most honored to meet you." In her bashed-up head, she searched her mother's etiquette teachings for advice about meeting royalty. She remembered only the bedtime animal tales, with wealthy toads, honey-loving bears, naughty rabbits, and wind-bag wolves.

Flora's head swirled. She had to do this right. No telling what the ruling rat would do to her if she used bad etiquette. Should she wave her tail, wiggle her ears, point her toes a certain way?

She shuffled her paws and dipped her head, which was about all she could do anyway in the snug space.

"Your honor, your macho, er, *majesty*, I hope I

drooped myself properly."

Her droop was more of a cringe. Aside from her discomfort from talking with a stranger, she felt foolish using royal words and gestures for a rodent smaller than herself. Especially one with such a spine-grating voice! And where was his crown? His scepter? And the royal robes? On the other paw, his glassy eyes and pompous nose *did* command some respect. Moreover, she *was* an accidental guest. In *his* royal home.

"Your gruesomeness, I beg your forgiveness for not knowing about kingly ways. And even more for my intrusion-ness. But honestly, I'm not sure how I got here and what I'm to do next."

King Cyrus stared at Flora. The white patch of fur above one eye lifted and the other one crinkled. "You crazy packrat. The first thing you should do is shake the rain off your befuddled behind."

She shook her head. Had she heard him correctly? Shaking her befuddled behind was another matter; it was so sore and bruised it hurt too much.

King Cyrus lowered his nose and grabbed a seed from a little pile. "You know, Flora," he smacked his mouth, "I don't let just anyone pop into my kingdom. But at least you were *sensible* enough to bring water."

"Oh, kind worthless…er, *worthiness*, you are so very welcome." She sighed and relaxed her tight whiskers. King Cyrus welcomed Flora's intrusion. The rain on her fur moistened the air in his palace, which would help keep him healthy and comfortable.

"So, you colossal packrat, you can stay a while and drip."

That's all she needed to hear. She was safe. This rat king was not kicking her out; and thanks to the Packrat on High, for she had never seen a pair of feet so big.

As she drifted into an exhausted sleep, one of his words kept bouncing around in her head. *Sensible.* That's what she was, sensible. She had a sensible life, a sensible home in the jangly-crate. She knew where and when to look for food and precious things. And she was sensible enough to avoid dangers, such as the demon cat and other evil beasts. And the dreaded cliff. Except now that she knew more about it, she dreaded it in a different way.

But would she ever see Grandma Mimi and Cousin Gertrude again, and feast on eggplants, and search for tasty treats in the munch mound? Would she even find her nest and snuggle with her precious things?

And the ancestral packrat home, why did her thoughts turn to the vision of a chain of packrats, all connected to that jumble in the crack in the cliff?

Flora dozed with these questions nudging her battered body and mind.

CHAPTER EIGHT
ESCAPING DEATH

"Flora, arise!" King Cyrus shrieked his command.

Flora reeled. "What...what is it?" She squinted, barely making out King Cyrus' beady eyes inspecting her face.

The recent events flashed through her head—the terrifying ride in the jangly-crate, the thunderstorm, hurling through the air, squirming into the royal palace occupied by the puny King Cyrus.

"Follow the king to the hinterlands! We must fill the royal coffers!"

"Huh? What? Um, your royal rat-ship...What? Royal cough? Hinter-*what*?"

"The hinterlands—the boondocks, backcountry, the wilderness! Off to the wilderness, we must go to gather seeds for the coffers—the royal pantry! Make haste!"

King Cyrus squeezed past her and crept along the passage to its opening. Flora sighed. She must obey the king, or else...well, she wasn't sure about the "or else" part, but she couldn't disobey. At the moment, she didn't seem to have a choice.

Feeling as though each paw was dragging a sack of dirt, she wormed after him, crying "*ohh*" and "*yikes*" and making throaty moans as she felt the bruises from her recent tumble.

The world had changed from the crazy one she had left a few hours earlier. Star dots spattered the night sky. Thin clouds smeared them away and streamed on. Light from a low waning moon outlined the sagebrush, silver buffaloberries, mountain mahogany bushes, and juniper trees, still dripping from the storm.

Sucking in the moist air, Flora looked up from the bottom of a canyon where rocky slopes, blotched with plants, rose on both sides.

King Cyrus bounded to a sagebrush, where he collected seeds and stuffed them into little pockets on his cheeks that seemed ideal for the task. Flora waddled after him. With little enthusiasm, she gathered seeds in her mouth. She didn't have special cheek pouches like his.

"Gather quickly. It will soon be light."

Flora looked for the jangly-crate but saw no sign of it. For now, she would help the king with the curious task of filling the royal coffers.

The night's seed gathering continued—around boulders, under skunkbushes and soaring trees, over decaying stems and leaves. They stopped only to collect the tiny seeds of fountain-like grasses.

Being a packrat, Flora spit out her mouthful of seeds to pick up an interesting looking twig. King Cyrus glared at her. Summoning all her willpower, she dropped the twig and gathered more seeds.

As they rounded the trunk of a cottonwood tree, she spotted another kangaroo rat on his haunches, stripping seeds from the spikes of feathery grass.

"Make way for the king!" his highness squeaked, thumping his powerful hind feet on the ground. The other kangaroo rat hardly gave notice. He kept filling his cheek pouches.

"I hereby command: make way, for King Cyrus cometh and wants to pass-eth!" More ground thumping challenged the other kangaroo rat.

"Yeah, yeah," the other rodent said with a tired sigh. He stood his ground, paused his work, and rolled his beady eyes at his king. "Greetings, your royal hiney, Ka-jing Cyrus." He winked at Flora.

Flora gasped. Surely the king would punish this sassy kangaroo rat. But with nose held high, King Cyrus sprang past him and cried, "Onward!" She followed, glancing back at the rude subject who seemed unimpressed by royalty.

By now seeds packed Flora's mouth. The king's full cheeks sagged. But the hunt continued around a cluster of boulders. Flora nearly smashed into the king's regal rump. He stood hunched and still, frozen like a tree stump.

Slobber! Snort! Huffa-puffa! A bulky animal slung damp earth past their heads.

"What is it?" Flora's words stuck in her mouth. Thick claws flashed.

"Hush! This brute will have us for breakfast." The king's squeaky voice tightened. "Badger. Don't even breathe."

Dirt stopped flying. The seeds in Flora's mouth felt like tiny rocks. Her stomach roiled. The black-nosed, gigantic head darted toward them. Gleaming eyes forced a cry from Flora. He lowered his striped face and moved a paw closer.

A mosquito buzzed by Flora.

"Danger! Run!"

Hopping and galloping, tubby rolls swishing, Flora chased the tail flag of King Cyrus as he bounded out of sight. Leaves crunched, twigs snapped as brutus badger pursued, his horny claws clickety-clacking.

"This way!" King Cyrus' guiding squeak steered her to a boulder, where she clambered to the trembling King Cyrus on top. *Clickety-clack, clickety-clack.* Below, a shadow snuffled, paused, and slipped into the darkness.

"Phew!" King Cyrus spewed seeds from his bulging cheeks.

Gulping hard, buzzing with fright, Flora moaned. An awful picture stuck in her head: packrat—badger snack; packrat—badger snack. So close. She moaned again.

As they recovered, stars faded and darkness lightened. Shadowy sandstone walls, streaked with black stains, rose high all around. A giant cage seemed to encircle her.

"I want to go home." The walls didn't answer.

A heavy silence hovered. Flora's heart felt hard and dull.

CHAPTER NINE
HANDSOME KING

"That fellow almost had us," King Cyrus announced. "The boundaries of my kingdom are near. We must move on!"

How could he keep going after their narrow escape? Flora couldn't manage another hop. Even so, she scrambled down the boulder after the king. His tufted tail trailed him in the lightening gloom. Flora could barely keep up. He did pause, every so often, to strip more seeds from grass tips. Only now they ended up strewn on the ground instead of packed into his ballooning cheeks.

"King Cyrus, your billowing cheekiness," Flora panted, catching up to him. "I beg for a rest. Don't you think we've done enough?"

Sitting upright on his springy hind legs, King Cyrus looked at Flora and cracked his mouth open. Scraps of green coated his teeth. His head sprouted sticky seeds of all sorts. The tiny claws on his front paws had skewered wads of seed hulls and grass blades. His eyes were all squinty next to his swollen cheeks, which looked like ripe eggplants, ready to explode.

"Oh, yes, yes, you're right, my dear," said the king, shaken from his frantic binge. "We've reached the boundaries of the kingdom. It's time to fill the royal coffers."

King Cyrus dug shallow holes one right after the other in the sandy soil. Into each, with a *putt-putt-putt*, he propelled seeds from his full cheeks, using his paws and shoulders to help push them out. He covered each hole with dirt. Within a few minutes, the king had given himself a facelift, erasing the cheek bulges. He looked like the kangaroo rat Flora remembered before their seed hunt.

But not for long.

"The royal coffers are filled!" With that declaration, King Cyrus threw himself on the moist earth. He rolled and wriggled until grit covered his fur. So shocked was Flora, she dropped all the seeds she had collected.

King Cyrus perched on his hind legs and cocked his dusty head at Flora, crinkling his pointy nose.

"Oh my, King Witless...I mean...wit-fulness, you're so...so...handsome." *What a silly thing to say*, she thought. But he did look, well, *silly* in his robe of grime. She couldn't tell the king he looked silly.

"Well, Flora the packrat, of course I am handsome." King Cyrus puffed up a bit and grew quiet, seeming to savor the thought of being a handsome king. "I say, what a jolly good subject. You're obedient and loyal, and serve the king with devotion." Despite her weariness and worries, Flora lightened. The king had given her a compliment. She must be using proper packrat—and kangaroo rat—etiquette.

"You have the makings of a brave knight of the realm. Why, I've never seen a packrat run so fast from a badger and capture so many seeds. Long live the kingdom! Long live King Cyrus!"

Flora's whiskers whirled as she basked in the king's words. But she remembered her dire situation and turned to the king to speak. Dirt rimmed his small ears, flecks of leaves flitted off his tasseled tail, and he puffed dust out his nostrils. In her imagination, his cheeks grew into big eggplants, and she had to stifle a giggle. What an un-kingly looking king.

Her heavy heart surfaced, wiping out her moment of distraction.

"King Cyrus, your grunginess." The king either ignored or excused her poorly chosen word. "I truly thank you for your kind words. But I don't want to be a knight of the realm. I just want to go home. I want to be with my treasures in my nest, and dig through the munch mound with my cousin Gertrude, and talk with Grandma Mimi again."

"Ahh, I see." The king seemed to grow thoughtful as he used his paw to push one last seed from his cheek pouch into his mouth. "A displaced subject. You are but a visitor here, and you seek your homeland."

"Yes, yes, that's it!" He seemed to understand her problem. Flora described her life at home, the terrifying ride in the jangly-crate, and separation from all she knew and loved.

"Can you help me find my nest, your grossness?" A long pause followed, agonizing for Flora because she had addressed the king with the wrong word.

"Very well. Flora the packrat, I shall help you find your jangly-crate and beloved nest. Now come along, my dear, back to the royal burrow we go!"

The world was a shade brighter. A flock of noisy piñon jays dipped overhead. Early morning chirps, rustles, and whooshes signaled the coming dawn.

CHAPTER TEN
WITNESS TO DEATH

Feeling lighter, Flora followed King Cyrus back to his underground castle. Along the way, near a clump of gramma grass bent with seeds, small footprints blanketed the moist earth. A narrow trench mysteriously appeared and disappeared among the prints.

"So many animals have been here. Look at all these tracks."

"Those aren't the tracks from other animals, you silly packrat, those are *your* tracks!"

Indeed, they were. Flora turned in the same

direction of travel of the footprints and jumped all four feet into them. A perfect fit. She followed her own prints, putting each paw in its matching track. But what was the shallow trench between the footprints? She winced. A snake had stalked her. Examining the squiggle more closely, she blinked her eyes and skipped off the ground.

"That was no snake. That was my tail!" Flora whapped her tail on the ground a few times, then compared those fresh marks to the ghostly marks she had left earlier.

"Oh look, your high nose, see my tail mark?" She turned toward King Cyrus, who had watched Flora's detective work with amusement.

But now the king's attention was elsewhere. His head was tilted back, and his whiskers barely flinched. Flora followed his gaze and her jaw dropped. High above in the shadows of a cottonwood tree peered a set of saucer eyes framed by a giant head of feathers. Dipping and jerking, its beak ripped the fur of an animal clutched in its sharp talons.

"Your royal fluffiness, what do we do?" She whispered, captured by the scene. A curtain of ice dropped on them both. The victim's lifeless tail and four paws—the rear pair much bigger than the front—dangled over the branch. The bird paused and blinked into the darkness, raised the prey clutched in a set of talons, and slid the limp form into its mouth. Flora and King Cyrus watched the long, tufted tail disappear.

"Oh my," she murmured, "the rude kangaroo rat." The king had lost one of his subjects to a great horned owl.

Flora jolted him from his stupor.

"Your highness, let's move!" Flora led the way. The king sprang after her. Although in strange territory, she followed the footprints and tail marks she had left earlier while gathering seeds. When the opening of the royal dwelling appeared, she herded the king through and scurried after him, deep into safety.

Wheezes and shivers filled the tiny earth cave as they huddled. King Cyrus pushed himself against the wall and hung his head in his paws, leaving only his drooping ears visible. Every so often a whisker shuddered. Flora's trembles relaxed, but the thick air made her gulp for freshness.

Dim eyes peeked over the king's paws. "My kingdom has lost a noble subject." He reached for a seed and chewed, staring.

A pang shot through Flora. The feisty king, who had bubbled with commands and vaulted through the kingdom, was now as flat as a dried-up cactus pad. Even though the owl's victim had not honored him, the king was grieving as though he had lost a blood brother.

And that grisly memory! She couldn't let it go. The yellow eyes, the pointy beak, the talons. She knew predators needed to eat animals like herself to live. That's just how it is, her mother had told her. But it could have been King Cyrus or herself up in the tree instead. Flora shivered.

First the badger, then the owl. Flora had out-run death and witnessed death, both within a few short hours. This new place was filled with dangers. In her old home, Flora knew the dangers and how to avoid them. Unlike this place—where she had never even heard of a badger before now. Likewise, she had never seen an owl swallowing a freshly killed animal. Who was still warm. Whom she had just met. Who had *winked* at her even.

My home isn't anything like this...But there's that beast—that killer that haunts the old packrat home. He ate the packrat babies, and he still drags victims there. Will I become his victim when I go home? Or...is this awful place going to be my new home?

She shook those thoughts away. Her stomach grumbled. Through all the recent happenings she had not eaten. Worried or not, she needed to find food.

Flora squirmed past King Cyrus, now staring at his front paws, moaning softly. She poked her ears past the burrow entrance into the rays of a rising sun. Rarely did she leave her nest during daylight, especially when she knew a murderer prowled close-by. But she wasn't in *her* nest. And in this strange place, she seemed to be doing all kinds of things differently.

"I smelled one here earlier," she mumbled and sniffed. "Aha, there it is." The perfume of a prickly pear cactus.

But the scent was muddled. She smelled something more interesting—an odor she knew from outside the two-legged rodents' bloated burrow, during evenings when the air crackled and bright flickers threw dancing shadows. Smoke, from a wood fire—unmistakable! Flora's mind raced. Smoke—fire—two-legged rodents—*her* two-legged rodents. Jangly-crate—nest—home.

"Home! It's close, I know it!" She trotted this way and that, searching around bushes and over rocks, but she couldn't find the fire, two-legged rodents, or jangly-crate. Lonely junipers, jagged boulders, tangled scrub oak, and skunkbush stood their ground, giving no hint of her former life.

Flora whimpered, gnawed a cactus pad, and sniffled. She dragged her paws back to the earth chamber, where she joined King Cyrus in slumber.

CHAPTER ELEVEN
FALSE STARTS

"The night unfolds. Come, Flora, the coffers, the royal coffers!" Flora scrunched her back, trying to shake off King Cyrus' squeals. He seemed to have cast off the grief that had gripped him earlier. When she remembered her search for the fire and jangly-crate she moaned.

"Here we go again," she muttered. *But maybe King Cyrus will find the jangly-crate. He did promise to help me,* she thought.

As they emerged from the burrow, scanning the skies for the taloned predator, they heard something strange. From a huge piñon pine tree, a weird song rose and fell, whistled and warbled, grew strong, and faded. It was unlike any bird chirrup, wind flutter, animal cry, or two-legged rodent chant Flora had ever heard.

"Oh my, that sound is so…so…*peculiar.*" It disturbed her but made her curious. "What is it, your groovy-ness? Do you think it will attack?"

"I think not. That fellow is in fine form this evening. Let's have a look." King Cyrus leaped on a boulder near the tree and squinted, waving his floppy front paw at Flora to join him.

From beside the king, she searched for the singer in the shadowed branches. She only heard his melody. Strangely enough, the music soothed her. Sweet notes trilled and slid and celebrated, causing Flora to float to places within herself that felt delicate and sad and beautiful. For an instant, she found that dark, empty place in her heart.

The world hung, expanding in stillness.

"Bravo! Bravo!" the king shouted, interrupting the silence. He drummed his hind foot, shouted again, then drummed his other hind foot. Flora opened her eyes, searching for the performer.

The pine limbs crackled. A hefty figure rumbled along a thick branch, then backed down the trunk. It hit the ground and plodded to the boulder where they sat. This animal was bigger than Grandma Mimi, bigger than the cat. It was nearly as big as a coyote, although Flora wasn't so sure because only once had she seen one of those.

"D—did, did you l—like it?" said a thin voice. King Cyrus and Flora looked at each other with wide eyes, then looked back at the animal.

"A bully fine job!" King Cyrus bounded down the boulder with Flora close behind.

They stopped short of the hunched-up ball of a creature. Long fur cascaded all over his body, hiding an inner blanket of stiff thick hairs.

"I j—j—just learned that one." Small eyes searched over his round black nose. Although wary of this scary-looking stranger, Flora wanted to say something to him.

"Your song was...uh..." She was staring at a pair of orange front teeth that curled like a crescent moon. "Uh, piercing...er...perfect."

"I've never heard a porcupine belt out such a grand musical performance." King Cyrus squeaked and cleared his throat. "You are an expert opera singer! I shall make you the official entertainer of the royal court. What is your name, dear fellow?"

"P—P—Paco, my, my name is Paco." Obviously pleased with the compliments, Paco lifted his face, squinted, and chattered his teeth.

King Cyrus puffed his scrawny chest and introduced himself, declaring he was "Cyrus—King of the Realm and All the Kangaroo Rats."

Flora recalled nothing in packrat etiquette about talking with a porcupine. *I'm probably supposed to stay away from such a spiny creature, but at least I should introduce myself.*

"I'm Flora. I'm only visiting. I've lost my home, temporarily. King Cyrus is going to help me find it." She managed a smile. "How did you learn to sing so beautifully, Mr. Paco?"

"I was n—never good at t—t—talking." Paco kept looking at the ground as he spoke. "My m—mother said I was b—born with a stutter in my t—teeth." He looked at Flora, who nodded. "But my m—mother said I c—came into the world singing."

Flora's eyes widened. "Well, we have something in common, Mr. Paco. My mother also told me how I came into the world—talking—and I never stopped!"

Paco chattered his teeth and squeezed his eyes into slits. "And I n—never stopped singing!" A sweetness warmed Flora's ears and nose as she looked at this shy creature.

"When I s—sing, I f—feel free!" His eyes grew dreamy. Raising his chinless mouth, he bellowed in perfect pitch with the sparkly evening, "Freeee!"

The outburst snapped all three to action.

King Cyrus bounded to a clump of feathery grasses yelping, "The coffers! The royal coffers!" Flora jolted for a prickly pear cactus. Paco strolled to a snakeweed bush and scraped the earth.

Sniff, crunch, chomp, smack. They scavenged for some time. Paco drifted to the piñon pine tree, where he scraped and gnawed the outer pine-scented bark, searching for the sweet sap-rich layer beneath. "Yum-yum yummy!" he sang with gusto. Hearing his happy outcry, Flora pranced a quick jig and fell to her old habits.

"These cactus pads are positively captivating this evening. Robust, well-balanced, velvety texture with a lingering aftertaste. The flavor is a bit daring but not too dangerous."

After stuffing her belly and clipping cactus spines for the royal burrow, Flora melted herself into the moonless sky, marveling at all the stars. *The same stars I see when I explore the munch mound. How is Gertrude doing with her three hungry pups? And is Grandma Mimi eating eggplants right now, remembering the old packrat home? The cliff, the dreaded cliff, the stolen pups...*

Something else—dark, silent—flew through her mind, or was it outside her mind? Did those stars grow dim for a second?

She cocked her head and sniffed, nose raised. Wood smoke. There it was again...the wood smoke of fire, of two-legged rodents, of the jangly-crate and her comfy nest. Home.

"Paco, King Cyrus, do you smell it? Smoke, from a fire." Both heard her excitement and drew near.

"By Jove, you are correct," the king squealed with alarm. "Fire! Fire in the kingdom!" With eyes wide, he pounded his hind feet, kicking up a cloud of sand. Flora zigged and zagged in front of his un-kingly eruption, trying to catch his attention.

Meanwhile, Paco watched as he nipped and chewed grass.

"Your dryness, er, blindness, I mean *highness*," Flora panted after they had both calmed down. "If I can explain, it's fire from the giant two-legged rodents—who have the jangly-crate with my nest. I must find it if I'm ever to return home. It must be nearby."

The king flapped his mouth noisily, cleared his throat, and sniffed. "Oh, of course, I knew that." He looked at Flora, who had tightened her mouth, pushing back a sob.

"Flora, I have not forgotten. You are a stranger here who has lost her way, and you seek the comfort of your mother country."

Flora's mouth trembled.

"And I shall help you."

"P—Paco is also at your s—service."

Flora nodded and oozed a few tears. "Thank you, both. I *do* feel like a stranger here, but I also know I have friends." All three shifted their bodies and looked at the ground.

"Now, where were we—oh yes, the smoke." Flora clicked them back to the task. They sniffed in all directions, trying to locate the smoke's origin.

"This way." The king pointed his nose.

"If I may differ with your liver...er, loftiness, it's *that* way."

"The king declares, it is *this* way!"

"Your bigness, er...sir monarch, your emperor-ness, the smoke is definitely coming from *that* direction." Flora's voice hardened a bit.

"The royal nose knows, and the royal nose knows it is this way!" His superior tone rubbed Flora in a raw spot. She was an expert at smelling wood smoke, and she knew what her nose knew, too.

"Oh, great raja rat, your warty-ness...er, worthiness, and shining ray of light." She went on with a touch of sarcasm. "Perhaps your divine schnozzle is a bit stuffy this evening. The smoke is coming from *that* direction." She was nearly out of words. And patience.

The king sputtered and puffed. He had no retort. They glared at one another, pushing their chins out, each sure of what they knew.

Crunch, scrape, chomp, crunch, smack, slurp, snort. They looked at Paco, who seemed to adore scraping piñon bark. Bits flew from his gnashing mouth as he waggled his head at them with enthusiasm.

Flora and the King faced each other again, chins lowered and eyes softened.

"Maybe I will *never* get home." Flora sighed.

King Cyrus and Paco looked at the withered Flora.

Holding his nose aloft, the king stamped his hind foot. "Never fear, Flora. We shall triumph."

"Yes. I f—feel it in m—my quills." Paco chattered his teeth.

"Thank you, your crone...er, groan...no, croon...er, *crown*! Thank you, Paco. I'm sure we will find my nest." *But,* she thought grimly, *even the rat king can't help me. And all that porcupine can do is sing. And eat.*

Hardly had she finished the thought when a gentle lullaby wrapped around her, like the trinkets in her nest in the jangly-crate. As Paco's soft notes melted, Flora felt stronger. With moist eyes she looked at her friends, then focused on the night sky, searching for the wood smoke again.

She felt no alarm, no panic, no sense of doom when she saw it. She just coolly stated, "There he is. Take cover."

Flora and King Cyrus scooted under a rock overhang. Paco plucked a grass blade and hummed. Hadn't he heard her warning? From beneath their cover, Flora and King Cyrus watched razor-sharp talons extend and curl. Outstretched wings silently flapped. A brief presence, a labored liftoff, and the great horned owl was gone.

A downy feather rocked, riding the still air.

CHAPTER TWELVE
CLUELESS

The feather hovered a breath away from Paco's nose. He eyed it as it drifted to the ground, then chomped and hummed as though nothing had happened.

King Cyrus flattened himself to the ground next to Flora, panting loudly. They had just avoided the fate met by the kangaroo rat the previous night.

In a shaky voice, Flora tried to reassure the king. "The owl has flown off, your greatness. He doesn't dare attack again as long as we stick close to Paco." But the squashed-out king stared, moaning.

Scanning above, Flora hurried to Paco, still eating grass. She shook her head. Their spiky companion could do *much* more than sing.

"Paco, you just drove off a big owl who wanted you for an evening meal. You know that, don't you?"

Paco stopped munching long enough to chant:

"Paco has a pleasant song,
But the audience, they don't stay long.
They get too close and catch a whiff.
It makes them gag; it makes them stiff.
They don't come back to hear my tune,
Because my BO makes them swoon."

"Oh, Paco, it's not your body odor, it's your quills. They'll hurt if you give an animal a face full of them."

Paco scrunched his face and wiggled, rippling his elegant hair and quills. "Hmm." He could say that without stuttering. "Hmm."

I can't believe he's clueless about the power of his quills! He does smell a bit ripe, but his quills are much more dangerous than his aroma. This opera-singing porcupine might as well be covered in earwax.

Flora shook her head again as she watched Paco munch.

Everything that had happened that evening—meeting Paco, smelling the wood smoke, disagreeing with King Cyrus, narrowly escaping the owl, and most of all missing her home—all of it had exhausted Flora. She needed to rest. But King Cyrus stayed fastened to the ground like a splat of sticky mud.

Flora tried to lure him from beneath the overhang. "Don't worry, your dashing gorgeous-ness, we'll be safe in the royal burrow."

King Cyrus stirred, grunted, and moved his hind legs, slithering on his belly until he raised himself upright. "Ah yes, I suppose." He kept looking at the sky as he shuffled his floppy feet.

"We'll search for my nest tomorrow, won't we?" Flora couldn't give up hope. After all, both Paco and King Cyrus had promised to help her. But so far they lacked success.

Paco answered Flora by rattling his head from side to side, losing a couple of quills. A corner of King Cyrus' mouth rose.

She coaxed King Cyrus back to his royal burrow while stars faded. On the way, Flora heard Paco singing. The melody brushed that dark lonely place in her heart with honey sweetness. But her home seemed further away than ever.

CHAPTER THIRTEEN
ODD THINGS

Hey, where's my squiggly treasure, the slicky roly-poly, the springy crazy quilt? Where am I? Flora awoke feeling fretful but mostly confused. She looked for the sticks and cactus pads and pebbles and shiny crumples in her nest in the jangly-crate. Instead, she smelled dirt and another animal. A tufted tail brushed her nose. She sneezed.

A wave of homesickness sloshed over her. *Gertrude, Grandma Mimi, I miss you.* They also would be moving on their nightly search for tasty morsels and interesting things to stash in their nests.

"Do they miss me? Do they even know I'm gone?" She tightened her mouth.

King Cyrus interrupted, squirming past her. "The coffers, the royal coffers!"

"Enough with the royal coffers. I just want my nest," Flora grumbled behind him.

The sagebrush, moistened by an earlier rain, filled the darkening air with a strong fragrance. Cool earth met Flora's padded feet as she gathered seeds. She avoided open spaces, where the owl could snatch her for an easy meal.

Flora listened for Paco's singing. She wasn't sure how he could help her get home, but he had promised. As King Cyrus drifted out of sight, she chomped some tender rabbitbrush shoots and moved to a prickly pear pad. "Oh, yum." Saying that always made it taste better.

But the oddest thing happened. Or maybe it wasn't that odd, given all the other unusual things that had happened recently.

The prickly pear cactus spoke. To her. She clearly heard it say, "Oh, so you like eating me, do you?"

She stopped chewing and leaned closer.

"Ouch! Don't bite me. That hurts. *Bad girl!*"

"What?" Flora's stomach was the boss when it

was hungry, so it told her what to say. "But I *must* eat you. I am hungry and thirsty, and you are my most favorite food." She hopped backward, cactus slime trailing from her mouth.

"What am I doing? I have never talked to a prickly pear cactus. I won't do it now. Besides, a talking plant is odd."

Her thoughts went wild. *What if it attacks? Those sharp spines… But it's a plant; it can't attack. I'm very good at not getting stuck by cactus spines. But plants don't talk, either. Why is it talking? Maybe my packrat etiquette is wrong.*

"Oh, so now I'm not juicy enough for you?"

"But you just said 'don't bite me.'" Flora's bossy stomach had taken over again, ignoring her vow not to talk to a plant. She backed up and crouched beneath a sagebrush.

"You're stepping on my toes, you paunchy packrat!"

Flora jumped so high she nearly slung herself around the branches of the complaining sagebrush. She scurried under a boulder, gulping and trembling.

"I'll protect you," the boulder said in a deep voice, "from the awful talking plants."

Flora ran into the open, something she naturally avoided doing, and twisted in tight circles, first one direction, then the reverse. She became so dizzy she collapsed. The world spun around her.

From the edges, she heard a peal of laughter. Again, another ripple of laughter, and it grew stronger. Head still spinning, Flora looked around, trying to pinpoint the source.

It's King Cyrus. He's laughing at me—he saw me, and he's laughing. But he was nowhere around. She was alone in her dizzies and growing nervous.

But she wasn't alone. The titters continued, louder now. She was sure the laughter was coming from the snakeweed bush at the edge of the clearing.

Gathering her wits and stability, she called, "Who is laughing? I demand to see you right now!" She had to end this misery.

The lowest branches of the snakeweed stirred. An animal shape appeared from its shadows and walked along the edge of the clearing. The giggles continued.

Flora knew this animal but had never talked to one. The tall upright ears, hesitating walk, the nose sniffing this way and that, the puffy white tail.

The cottontail rabbit walked closer to Flora,

who had watched its every move with suspicion. Obviously, the rabbit had been laughing at her.

"Forgive me, packrat, but that was so much fun. I couldn't help myself. Sometimes I get carried away." The bright, upbeat voice startled Flora.

"Well, *you* would be confused, too if plants and rocks talked to *you* out of the blue." Flora's nostrils flared.

The rabbit squelched another giggle.

"I *love* your tail. So bushy and long, such an *adorable* squiggle. And it follows you around so sweetly!" Flora jumped. The voice came from right behind her. Someone had been examining her rump while she was talking with the rabbit.

The rabbit collapsed on its back and rolled, mouth open and paws scratching the air. Overcome with mirth, it wheezed and snorted between gleeful hoots.

This was one rabbit Flora should ignore. *How rude! Voices everywhere scaring me silly, even insulting me, plants yelling at me, and I'm doing a jerky dance like a goofball. And the rabbit thinks it's hilarious! This rabbit needs a good dose of...of... packrat etiquette.*

Flora firmed her jaw and sniffed, holding back a tear. She would stand her ground.

The rabbit sat up, eyed Flora's twisted face,

and stopped laughing.

"Oh, come over here, packrat, and get yourself out of the bull's-eye of some hungry animal." The rabbit was no dummy. Flora had made a fool of herself in an open area where the owl or another predator would have easy pickings. Holding her head high, she walked under the brush cover to the rabbit.

"What's your name, packrat? My name is Dayana. To most animals around here, I'm Dayana the Fabulous." The rabbit stared at Flora with a goofy grin. Flora tightened her mouth, jutting her jaw and raising her muzzle. This rabbit, fabulous or not, had treated her oh-so-rudely. Packrat etiquette called for avoiding talk with someone who treats you oh-so-rudely. But if you do talk, etiquette called for *clever*, rather than *polite* talk.

"Why 'Fabulous'? What's so fabulous about a rabbit who laughs at other animals? I think you should be 'Dayana the Fiendish'—that's another word for evil, in case you didn't know, and if you don't like that one, I can think of a bunch of even better words. Like nasty. And wicked. And foul. And *maladextrous*." She had no idea if "maladextrous" was a real word, but it sure sounded perfect, even clever, to throw at this smart-alecky rabbit.

By the time she finished her lecture, Flora's anger had lost steam.

They each stared at the other. Dayana's eyes danced. Flora's jaw softened. Whiskers on both trembled. Flora looked at the ground and back at Dayana.

"Flora. That's *my* name, just plain Flora."

Flora the packrat and Dayana the rabbit each cracked a timid smile, and both knew they would become fast friends.

CHAPTER FOURTEEN
MAGIC

"The royal coffers are filled!" King Cyrus galloped to the edge of the clearing and skidded to a stop when he saw the two forms huddled in the shadows. "Who goes there in the king's realm?"

"Your super-duperness, it's me and Dayana—Dayana the Fabulous."

"Fabulous? *Fabulous?* Who is so fabulous who stands before the mighty Cyrus, King of the Realm and All the Kangaroo Rats?" He moved closer.

Dayana looked like a naughty imp ready to

play a joke on someone. Even on a king. But she did not move or speak.

"What mighty king is this bubble-headed rat-like thing who squeaks through his tail tuft?" The king squeaked a gasp and glanced behind him.

"What? Who said that? Show yourself now, or I'll have you boiled in skunk oil! I'll have you flown at half-mast! I'll have you bonkered!" He looked this way and that but found only the rabbit and the packrat emerging from the shadows.

Dayana the Fabulous twittered. Wide-eyed Flora looked at her, then understood. This rabbit had powers—*special* powers she used to scare the wits out of others. Magic! Of course, how could she have been so dim-witted? The rabbit had used magic to make the plants and rock talk to Flora earlier. If she could do that, then this rabbit could use magic to make the jangly-crate with her nest appear so she could go home.

With growing excitement, Flora whispered to Dayana, "Careful, he's a bit, ah, different. You should tell him about your magic powers now." Dayana looked at the king while growing a daffy grin.

"Oh noble King of the Realm and All the Kangaroo Rats, your courage and wit and good looks are known throughout the land."

The king lifted his nose, expanded his chest, and rippled his whiskers. "Of *course* I am good looking, and those other things," he squeaked. "*Who* said that?"

Dayana had not moved her mouth, except when she strained it shut to keep from howling with laughter. Even Flora, who was amazed that this rabbit *was* truly, magically, *fabulous*, looked down to hide her amusement.

"I spoke, your royal suaveness. I am most honored to meet you." Dayana bowed her head low, stifling a snicker. *Thanks to the Packrat on High*, Flora thought, *Dayana understands this meeting needs a serious tone.*

"Well, for crumpet's sake. So it was you, rabbit? Indeed!" The king stared at her, then glanced behind himself to make sure no one else was there.

"But I prefer mink oil if your royal-ship doesn't mind." Something seemed weird. Dayana's mouth hardly moved a hair—it was frozen instead in a toothy grin. But the voice definitely came from her mouth.

The king's jaw dropped while the pair of white patches above his eyes rose high with delight. "By Jove, this sure takes the biscuit! We have an actual ventriloquist in our midst." He waved his front paws. "Yes, by golly, an honest-to-goodness ventriloquist! Why, I shall name you, 'Dayana the Fabulous, court jester.' Court jester you shall be!" The king drummed his hind foot.

"If I might ask, your grapey-mess, er, graciousness, what did you call her?" Flora had figured it all out, but now she was confused. "Ben-trill-of-kids?"

"Ven-tril-o-quist. She is an expert at disguising and throwing her voice. A good ventriloquist can make anything appear to talk but without moving her mouth. Dayana is so good at it, she even fooled the great King Cyrus." The great king chirped a laugh.

Dayana exploded in laughter, for she had contained it too long. After she wiped a tear she sputtered, "Forgive me, but sometimes I crack myself up."

With a mournful smile, Flora asked, "So you don't know magic?"

"No, but it looks magical, doesn't it?" Dayana grinned so broadly her tall ears crossed on top of her head.

Flora sighed. No magic powers. No jangly-crate. No going home.

The king saw Flora's dismay. He explained to Dayana that Flora was lost from another kingdom, and he had promised to help her get home.

"The poor thing. She shouldn't be so unhappy. We must work together to help her get home." Dayana turned to Flora and put a rabbit's foot on her furry shoulder. "Don't worry, Flora. See how the king and I are here to help you? We'll figure it out somehow."

Encouraged by the words of her new friend, Flora nodded.

From afar, a melody slid over boulders, drifted around juniper branches, and stroked their ears.

"Paco," Flora whispered. She motioned her companions to follow as she scurried by rabbit-brush and furrowed cottonwood tree trunks until she came to the same piñon pine tree where she had first heard that magnificent performer.

They sat and listened, scarcely breathing, to pure sweetness filling the canyon.

When echoes of the last notes drifted away, all three pounded their hind legs while the king cried, "Bravo! Bravo! A beautiful aria!" Dayana's ears crossed. Flora wiped a tear and sighed, in a good way. She had forgotten for a short while she was in a strange land, far from her old familiar life.

Paco climbed from his tree stage and lumbered his pincushion body toward them. Dayana gulped. Her big eyes bulged even bigger. She stepped back for every step Paco moved forward. He stopped, Dayana stopped, and Paco looked at Flora.

"You s—see? My B—BO," moaned Paco.

Oh, brother. Flora shook her head. *This porcupine is hopeless.*

"No, Paco, it's your *quills*, remember? Your quills—they're sharp and can damage someone. Dayana here knows you could skewer her."

"Hmm." Paco seemed puzzled.

"Hmm," said Dayana. "Something's wrong with this picture. Flora, what's wrong with this picture?"

Flora whispered to Dayana, explaining how Paco thought his body odor scared other animals rather than his quills. Dayana nodded as she eyed the prickly singer.

"Paco, this is Dayana the Fabulous. She's going to help me get home, too." Chattering his teeth, Paco looked at the rabbit and plucked a blade of grass with his long claws.

"Your singing is divine, oh thorny one." A syrupy voice seemed to come from King Cyrus. The voice was totally unlike his usual squeaks and unbecoming from such a regal rat.

Paco stopped chewing and squinted at the king's face.

Dayana elbowed Flora and laughed.

"Oh, Paco, Dayana did that. She's fabulous because she can throw her voice and make anything talk. She's a trillforkiss."

"Ven-tril-o-quist," said the king.

Dayana showed her skills to Paco, making nearly every flower, rock, and leaf say something in its own special voice while her mouth stayed still. She even made Paco's quills trade mean insults with each other.

Paco bellowed, "Fabuloso!" in his best singing voice. Dayana giggled, crossing her ears and infecting them with her joyful spirit.

Their laughter faded, leaving them in the music of the canyon night. A gang of insects seemed to be blowing tiny whistles, trying to out-trill one another. Nighthawks dive-bombed, slicing the air with their whooshing wings. Dried leaves crinkled under the skitter of tiny animal claws. And from far down the canyon, a low "ho-ha-hooo, hoo-ho" drifted their way. Shivering, they made sure they were hidden under brushy cover. The owl seemed far away, but they needed to stay alert.

In the company of her three friends, Flora felt something stirring deep within her. That dark empty place in her heart, the place she glimpsed when she learned about the ancient packrat home, was rising, rising inside. When she thought about these strangers-turned-friends, who promised to help her get home, lumps grew and clogged her throat, and even tried to get into her eyes as tears.

Her other life tugged at her. The jangly-crate and her precious nest were like a far-away dream; she wasn't even sure what they looked like anymore. Gertrude and Grandma Mimi and the munch mound and the eggplant treats and the dreaded cliff with the packrat home in the crack—all were images she fought to hold in her mind. It seemed like forever since she had left.

Her friends seemed to sense her heaviness. All at once, three pairs of dark eyes rested on her face. Flora sighed, swallowing hard to keep the throat lumps down, and silently shared her sad feelings.

"We shall go on a scouting mission," the king declared. "We must search far and wide for Flora's nest."

The king sprang out of sight, leaving Flora dazed and with no time to disagree, even politely.

Paco clamped his mouth onto the bark of a scraggly piñon pine tree and gnawed, making happy chompy sounds. Flora sniffed, hoping to smell the smoke from the two-legged rodents' fire. She smelled only the earthy coolness of summer drawing to a close.

Her stomach growled and she moved to a clump of cactus pads. Dayana followed and pulled on some grass blades. Flora felt content with her new friend.

"Dayana," she said as cactus snot dribbled from her mouth, "how did you learn that amazing trick you do—that ventriloquist thing?"

"Oh, something I learned from my great-uncle. He learned from his grandfather, who was the last of a clan who perfected the craft."

"So are there other rabbits who do it?"

"There *were* others. I'm the last. None of my family wanted to learn—they wanted to eat." Dayana grew quiet as she seemed to be thinking about her great-uncle. "He teased me all the time with his different voices. I begged him to teach me, but he said the craft was only for the male clan. He had promised on his grandfather's foot to teach only his sons."

"So what happened?" Flora's mother had taught her oodles about packrat etiquette, expecting her to teach her own future pups, whether they were sons or daughters.

"I tricked him one day." Dayana chuckled. "I figured out the basics. I made a saucy lady rabbit lure him into a bush. He got all excited, dove in, and found a turtle."

"Wasn't he angry, Dayana?"

"Nah, not my great-uncle—he thought it was a clever joke. That's when he knew I had natural talent, and he taught me all the secrets. We used to team up and make our relatives seem to talk in weird voices."

"I think it's magical, what you do," said Flora between munches. *I wish she could magically send me home*, she thought.

"Yes, it's entertaining. Makes me sad I couldn't pass the craft on to others in my family." Dayana chewed some more and turned to Flora. "Would you like to learn how to do it, Flora? It isn't that difficult. You just need to learn some skills and special tricks."

Flora's eyes brightened. Learning how to be a ventriloquist sounded interesting. It might even keep her mind off her homesickness. "Do you think I could learn how to make those funny voices? And make bushes and rocks talk?"

"Sure, even a chunky packrat can do more than eat." The cactus spoke again. Dayana's mouth was still, but her ears were crossed as she looked at Flora.

Flora rolled her eyes. "Just teach me how to make the plants talk, please. And I'm not a chunky packrat if you don't mind. I'm a *goddess*."

"Of course. Let's begin. Remember, it's an illusion. It looks as if the plant is talking because you—the real talker—aren't moving your mouth. And you trick the audience into hearing the words a certain way. First, you need to practice making the different sounds without moving your mouth."

Practice Flora did, over and over. At first, she said words and phrases that needed only a little mouth-moving, such as, "Into the night I took a rat king strolling," and "Night and day again I stray, into the gray, not to say this is okay, so on this day I say hooray, eh?"

Next Dayana taught her to say more difficult words like "bug" and "mud" and "fickle" and "pickle" by making similar sounds and saying them quickly. Once she got the hang of it, Flora could say, "The king and I made prickly pear pie and had a big fun party," without hardly moving her mouth.

Flora and Dayana grabbed each other's front paws. They twirled, hopped, and tripped over one another as they sang but didn't appear to sing:

"The rabbit and the packrat,
Pranced around the tree,
And looked and looked for berries,
But fell and scraped their knees!"

"But that's not all. Now you need to learn how to *throw* your voice so that yucca fruit over there will talk." Dayana showed Flora how to speak from way back in her throat and to use her belly to project her voice into crevices and onto sticks and rocks and stumps. After a lot of practice, Flora improved her ventriloquist skills.

"You're getting pretty good at this, Flora."

"Really? So did I flummox you? Flabbergast you?" She loved the sound of those words. Romping in circles she sang, without moving her mouth, "Flora can flummox a king!" and "Flora the famous flabbergaster!" Dayana threw her head back with her ears crossed and snorted, falling with Flora in a heap.

But the happiness soon ended. Shadows waved under the four-wing saltbush nearby. Flora caught the movement from the corner of her eye. She clutched Dayana. With whiskers taut, both froze and squinted, fearing they had attracted something that smelled them as a warm juicy dinner.

CHAPTER FIFTEEN
MISSION REPORT

"What is it?" whispered Flora, practicing her motionless mouth skills. Her teeth chattered.

"Don't know." Dayana didn't move her mouth either. Feeling numb, Flora squeezed Dayana harder.

The bush boomed with a hollow voice. "There lurks a chill in summer's air...Good heavens! It's someone's derrière!"

Flora cried out and jumped straight up.

"That's French for 'butt,'" Dayana said flatly.

She flopped on her back, clamped her face in her front paws, and howled and gulped for air, overcome by her joke.

From the shadows ambled Paco and King Cyrus. Paco snorted and chattered his teeth. King Cyrus strode on his bouncy legs, flashing an un-kingly grin.

Paco sang out, "Derrière!" using a strong French accent.

Dayana, still on her back, blurted, "Flora sure was the butt of that one!"

Amidst hiccups of squeaky titters, King Cyrus said, "I say, my ventriloquist court jester knows some splendid jokes. Derrière, indeed."

Flora could barely stop her frightened teeth-chattering. In wide-eyed disbelief, she stared at her friends behaving like silly young pups—at her expense. King Cyrus stifled his titters and Dayana rolled to her feet. All of them looked at Flora.

Flora could hardly move her mouth. "I don't, I don't see what..." Her voice broke. She wanted to lecture them on their thoughtless joke. *After all, they know I'm not happy in this scary place, and I miss my nest and...*She saw their furrowed brows, their looks of concern. The lumps from the dark deep rose, and this time they went to her eyes. She didn't try to push them back, she dribbled tears and the lumps shriveled like little balloons. After a few moments, she sighed and smiled a little.

All of them shifted and shuffled their feet, and breathed more easily.

King Cyrus cleared his throat. "I have a mission report." He looked at Flora with white eye patches crinkled. "I detected smoke from a fire. However, I was unable to pinpoint its location. I also heard noises—banging and clanking, like things dropping on rocks, and strange animal-like sounds, in no particular pattern. The noises seemed far away, but they could have been close."

Flora's heart leaped. The two-legged rodents were still around! The king heard the same noises she had heard the day she was taken from her previous life.

"The sounds must have come from the two-legged rodents in the jangly-crate, your wistful wise-ness, er, wise one," Flora said. "If I can ask, where were you when you smelled the smoke and heard the noises?"

King Cyrus pointed his nose toward the top of the high canyon walls. His voice trailed as he said, "Up there, way up there, as far as this kingly body could go, to the outermost edges of the kingdom, where, I daresay, no rat has ever gone before."

His distant tone suggested the danger and great strength needed for his travels. Flora and the others moved from beneath a rabbitbrush to get a better look at "way up there." There was no end—piles of boulders, sheer vertical walls, layers on layers of sandstone, drop-offs and overhangs, hidden ledges where ravens tucked their young and spilled whitewash down the canyon face.

Where, exactly, did all the noises come from way up there? Which side of that vast canyon? On the top, way back from the edge, or behind one of those boulders as big as the two-legged rodents' bloated burrow? In one of those jaggy cracks that split the canyon wall where water spilled, leaving a trail of stones and bent shrubs?

Where, exactly, had Flora's journey begun that stormy night? What path took her to the opening of the king's palace? Flora could barely see the canyon edge where it met the sky. She couldn't climb to the top—and even if she made it, she might be in the wrong place, or on the wrong side.

"We must go up, Flora. I'm sure we will find the jangly-crate with your nest." Dayana wiggled her cottontail.

Paco sang a fluttering song, and Flora felt herself rising with the notes from the canyon floor all the way to the top, where she bounced back and forth between the canyon walls on the song's echo.

Her hopes soared. "Yes, we *must* go up." Dayana had said *we* not *you*. With her friends' help, she could not fail. She would make the journey despite the distance and energy needed. "I know the jangly-crate is there with my nest, so I can get back to—"

But Flora was speaking to no one. King Cyrus and Dayana had scattered willy-nilly. Paco was clawing the dirt for roots.

Uh-oh. This is not good. In an instant, her hope drained away and she felt exposed and alone. She looked up to see a moving shadow—blotting away the stars, squeezing the air on top of her head.

Flora shut her eyes, preparing for the worst.

CHAPTER SIXTEEN
COLLISION

Whoosh! Whoosh! Fluttering, thrashing. Flora's fur rippled. A piercing screech froze her blood.

Eyes squeezed shut, she listened to herself puff.

"Oh my, I guess I'm no more. But I can open my eyes, so I guess I *am* more." She popped open one eye, saw her pointy clawed toes, and opened the other, dreading what else she might see.

Paco stood beside her, head facing the opposite direction. His thorny tail was raised but then slapped the ground. Nearby the great horned owl wriggled and flopped, face turned away. Although upright on its feet, it pounded the ground with one wing stretched out at an odd angle. Its body leaned to one side.

Flora hopped backward; her ears and whiskers and fur pulled her back even more. The owl was so close, so big. It turned its giant head and the yellow saucer eyes looked right at her. They blinked. And blinked again. Those enormous eyes glowed with fear. The owl stopped trying to move.

Flora wanted to run. Far away. Get away from those sharp claws, the dreadful beak, those eyes boring through her head. But her paws stayed rooted.

The owl was injured. And Paco, dear Paco, had something to do with it.

"What h—happened?" Paco looked at Flora.

Without breaking her gaze at the owl, Flora whispered, "You did it, Paco, you used your power. The owl has your quills in its wings. It can't fly. You saved me from becoming its dinner."

Paco turned his stickery body around to face the owl along with Flora. By faint starlight, they saw the tips of a cluster of his long quills piercing the underside of the owl's wing, keeping it from folding the wing or flying away.

The owl glanced at Paco then attached its steady gaze on Flora. Its horny beak parted ever so slightly.

Flora and Paco stood as though in a dream. This meeting was not supposed to happen. Moments before, the owl was a hunter in the sky, searching for prey and seconds from grabbing a plump packrat off the ground. In a flash, the story turned on itself. The hunter instead collided with a porcupine, bringing it to earth. Paco, Flora, and the owl were now in a tense meeting where questions hung in the air: Was there still a hunter? Was there still prey?

From the bushes, Dayana slithered on her belly. King Cyrus shuffled on his big hind feet. They all gathered together—the four ground-dwelling animals and the owl, who now seemed one of them. All on the ground, all exposed to danger, all sharing this spot at the bottom of this big canyon. Beside one another, whiskers of the four friends relaxed. But the stillness became unbearable in that odd scene and King Cyrus spoke.

"That was a most daring action." He tried to sound confident, but his squeaky voice broke. "I shall make you a knight of the kingdom."

"Yes, I saw it all. You were so brave." Dayana spoke more loudly.

Paco blinked when he seemed to realize he had downed the powerful bird—not with his BO, but with his quills.

"Your tail hit its wing at the right second," said Dayana. "You saved Flora for sure."

Paco's handsome cheeks swelled and his quills stood erect. He hummed and opened his mouth in the happy cheer of a full-grown porcupine.

The owl fluttered and flapped, and squawked weakly. Dragging its talons, it tried to balance its body with the bent wing on one side.

Flora looked at its sad eyes. They were focused on her.

She thought it was the breeze, whistling through the piñon pine needles. *It's Dayana, making another joke. No, even Dayana knows this is no time for a joke.*

It was the owl. The owl was whispering to her. But she wasn't hearing it. She was *feeling* the whisper—not with her fur, not with her whiskers, but she was feeling it, knowing it in her head. Those piercing saucers were sending her a message. At first, Flora couldn't believe it. She shook her head and heard Dayana say, "What is it, Flora? What is it?"

But those eyes held her captive; they begged her to listen and accept what she felt, accept what she heard in her head.

I am hurt. And you live.

"Oh, oh my. The owl is *talking* to me."

CHAPTER SEVENTEEN
OWLS CAN'T TALK

"I don't hear anything." Dayana shook her head. "That owl can't talk. Everyone knows owls can't talk."

"But it's telling me something. I definitely heard it."

Dayana, Paco, and King Cyrus all turned their ears toward the owl, trying to hear what Flora was hearing. The owl's eyes widened but stayed focused on Flora.

I was hungry, little packrat, but now you live.

Flora cocked her head and squinted. "Did you

hear that?"

"Definitely not, you crazy packrat!" King Cyrus flapped his mouth. "You are imagining things. This beast is an invader of the kingdom who murders my innocent subjects. It has finally been conquered. It won't dare speak before its conquerors. And besides, everyone knows owls can't talk."

Paco bonked his tail on the ground. He nodded in agreement with Dayana and King Cyrus.

"Begging your forgiveness, your sage-ness, but I know what I heard, and that owl was talking to me in my head. I can *feel* it talking. And it wants me to listen."

Dayana and the king exchanged a worried look. Paco was still basking in the glory of having saved Flora from the now helpless bird.

"Owl, you are speaking to me, aren't you?"

Owl's eyes grew a hair wider; the feathers on its face rippled.

Open your heart, packrat. Hear me.

Flora moved closer to the owl. Those saucer eyes were melting her normal caution, but she did not dare move within batting distance of its wing. She could see the wounds. Tiny droplets of red beaded at the base of each quill. The owl parted its beak and softened its gaze.

We are one, you and I.

The owl seemed to be giving up, surrendering. She could not ignore those words because they were growing louder inside her head.

What a magnificent creature. Her mother had taught her to fear owls, but now she was admiring the razor-sharp talons, the feathers that made no sound in flight, the head that could turn on its flexible neck in a near circle. This animal could hear the scamper of creatures under leaves, see clearly over long distances, and carry prey much heavier than itself.

Little packrat. Know your strength.

"I *am* imagining things."

The owl shuffled, extended its unhurt wing, and blinked its eyes, seeming to disagree.

"Careful!" cried Dayana. "It will grab you!"

"Get back, Flora." The king thumped his foot. "Paco must finish the job, and free us from this monster." Paco grunted and slapped his tail.

"But don't you see? The owl can't hurt us." The words tumbled from Flora. "It's injured and knows it's in serious trouble. It's not an evil monster. It was doing what it does to be an owl."

The owl's eyes relaxed into a soft glow.

Flora swelled with confidence. She stepped close to the owl, nearly nose to beak. "I hear you, owl."

The owl's eyes fluttered.

"I know you need help."

The owl's eyes blinked. *You know more than you know, packrat.*

She shook her head. "Know more than you know?" Huh? *I know I'm just a packrat. I know this owl nearly snatched me. And now it's on the ground talking to me.*

Flora wriggled and squirmed as the owl returned her gaze. She was pressed to an edge, a dangerous place, an unknown place, a place where up meets down, in becomes out, black seems white, and there was no sure path. Ears trembling, she closed her eyes and tried not to think.

In that still dark place, she knew. At least she *thought* she knew, but she didn't have to think to know. Somewhere deep down, the path was clear. She turned to her friends and raised her head.

"I am going home. Owl is going to help. But we must accept that owl belongs here. We need to help it."

Paco, Dayana, and King Cyrus all drew back at Flora's crazy words. Their mouths dropped open.

Flora was not surprised by their reaction. "Alright then." A little nervous, Flora met the owl's eyes and thought her message to the owl. *Yes, we are one, owl. I want to go home as much as you want to live.*

Brave packrat, I salute you!

Flora disappeared under the crooked wing of that magnificent creature.

CHAPTER EIGHTEEN
STRENGTH OF GRATITUDE

A chorus of protests rang out.

"Flora, no!"

"Cease, I command you, stop at once!"

"N—NOOOO!"

She heard those cries, but Flora went to work. Using her teeth and paws, she grabbed and pulled the quills stuck in the flesh of the wing. Grunting, she yanked them one by one with all her might. But with each tug the owl flinched, tightening its wing muscles to protect itself from the pain.

After a few minutes, Flora was panting. She had removed only a few quills, with a big cluster left to go. The tiny barbs on the ends of the quills held fast in the owl's tensed wing.

"They're stuck," she moaned. "I don't know how I can do this, owl."

But a sweet song, softened by the hairs of the owl's feathers, flowed around her. Paco, dear Paco, was singing a soothing lullaby. Flora relaxed and the owl grew drowsy.

She yanked on another quill. This time the owl barely flinched and the quill loosened. Flora pulled another. Success! *Stay calm owl, I'll have them out in no time.* But after removing several more, the owl tightened again and held on to the quills, despite the sweetness of the lullaby.

The owl's wing moved, startling Flora. She was not alone.

"Flora, your bravery is smashing. I have come to assist." Good King Cyrus joined her in the wing cavity of the kingdom's invader.

"Your soft serve, I mean your sogginess. Oh, thank you!"

King Cyrus rocked on his big hind feet next to Flora and tugged on a quill. Together they made progress in removing the stubborn quills.

Meanwhile, the lullaby continued, easing

their work. The owl shifted into a dreamlike state, hardly moving.

But just then, outside the owl wing, strange voices bounced—as though a crowd of sarcastic, self-centered youngsters had gathered.

"Where'd you get that barnacle beak, owl?"

"Hey, would you dim those saucer eyes? They're ruining my complexion."

"If your head was any bigger, I could pop it like a puffball."

Dayana! She was using her different voices to distract the owl as they plucked its wing. Flora wasn't sure it was helping.

But something *was* working. She and King Cyrus, with gentle and steady work, removed all the quills. The wing oozed with speckles of fresh blood.

With mouths and paws numb from all the tugging, they backed out from under the feathered shelter and sucked in the cool air. Paco's lullaby faded, Dayana's insults stopped. Flora looked at the owl's closed eyes.

A slit widened in one eye, then the other, until those yellow eyes fixed on Flora. Gratitude from the owl spilled through her ears and tail and traveled to that deep dark place in her heart, giving it a little light. A smile crept on to her face.

Brave packrat, you shall find your home. Remember.

Thoughts breezed through Flora's body and trailed away. *Find my home? This place feels like a home.*

The owl folded its wounded wing, closed its eyes, and fell into a deep sleep.

Paco and Dayana tiptoed forward, joining Flora and King Cyrus. Side by side, in the day's first light, the four friends looked upon the slumbering, feathered giant.

CHAPTER NINETEEN
IT IS TIME

The four backed away, silent with their thoughts. Paco and Dayana faded into the brush. Flora and the king scampered back to his castle, grabbing a few mouthfuls of seeds and cactus pads.

The tunnel to the king's cloister was squishy tight. The damp walls smelled dirty-earthy. The king had carried away the cactus spines and twigs Flora had smuggled in for decoration and comfort. As she squirmed deeper, she felt like she was invading a place where she did not belong.

Thoughts of getting home followed Flora into

her dreams, where she became like a queen bee, creating whatever she desired She commanded yellow saucer eyes to light up the best packrat home ever, filled with glittering treasures and the scent of a bunch of other packrats. All the empty spots in her heart filled with fountains of color and anything seemed possible. She could even fly.

"Oh my!" Flora awoke with a jolt.

The owl eyes had a message. She dipped back into that dream world and searched. But it was unclear.

Remember, Flora. Remember...remember...remember what?

Remember the cliff, Flora. Remember the cliff.

Those words pierced her like a crack of lightning.

The cliff! The cliff! The packrat home, where her ancestors had lived, where her packrat family began, where they all created a big story. She had never set one paw in that place, but her heart was there. Likewise, that great packrat birthplace had squirmed into the deepest part of her heart. They were each within the other.

The burrow squeezed around her. An odor of urine scratched her nostrils. King Cyrus snorted. Flora shifted, tightening her muscles, twitching her toes.

"Your amazing-ness, er, delightful-ness, er, King Cyrus."

King Cyrus rustled and cracked one eye open. "Oh yes, the royal coffers," he muttered. "Is it time?"

"It is time!"

CHAPTER TWENTY
A FUZZY PLAN

Whoosh! Flora slithered from the grip of the underground burrow and met fresh air, damp earth, and strong smells. Raindrops darkened the trunks of the sagebrush and shimmered on the branches. The sky glowed pink, then turned grey as clouds brought the night.

"Hmm, so fragrant, so juicy," she murmured as she slobbered over her favorite food. But her tiny clawed toes twitched and vibrated, begging for action. Instead of helping King Cyrus with his usual seed search, she collected objects—lots of them. Her work wasn't packrat habit or packrat etiquette. For some reason, she *had* to gather these things.

By the time King Cyrus had returned from his nightly chores, Flora had a tower of cactus spines, fibers from yucca leaves, flexible twigs, and shreds of juniper and sagebrush bark.

"I say, what on earth are you doing, you crazy packrat?" King Cyrus eyed Flora through the grit of his dirt bath.

She didn't know what to say. The mound of canyon litter puzzled her also. "Tidying up, your cleverness." The mess was turning into a sculpture of sorts. But of what, she wasn't sure. Flora examined the pile and jutted her chin. "This isn't right." She tugged some yucca strands, unraveling the creation.

"Flora, your behavior is befitting of a befuddled packrat." King Cyrus licked his paws. "If you recall, last night I risked royal life and limb. I climbed steep and slippery slopes. I braved the frightening unknown to find that thing you call a jangly-crate where you have your nest. I even pulled quills from the wing of an invader of the kingdom. We must not lose time, but continue with the task of returning you to your homeland."

"Yes, your klingon, er, king-ness." Flora pulled

strands of grass tangled in a pine cone. "You were most magnificent last night, and dashing as well." The king smiled and swelled.

"But I have a plan." Flora was lining up strips of juniper bark. "And with your help, I think I can get to the jangly-crate." Flora didn't have a plan—that she could explain, anyway. It was still fuzzy. But she did sense a greater purpose behind her need to gather these odds and ends. "Aha! I need more bark shreds."

She yanked more shaggy strips from a juniper tree. King Cyrus joined her, bounding from the tree to the pile with clumps of bark. He ripped strands of yucca fiber, cut ribbons of grasses, and sprinkled juniper berries on the heap.

They were gathering materials needed to create a new packrat nest. But the purpose of their work, in fact, was something else.

The night wore on as the two rodents toiled. They hardly noticed the air turning thick and heavy, the sky growing dark and starless, the wind fluttering their ears. Flora needed to continue gathering.

"Help! Let me out! I can't breathe!" A voice wailed from the hodgepodge of materials.

Horrified, Flora ran around the pile. She had buried some creature. Horror turned to panic as the wee voice multiplied into a pack of voices. They kept moving around the pile. Had she smothered an entire family?

"Hey, that looks like a tasty feast." Dayana emerged from the bushes, grinning and flouncing her cottony tail. Flora sighed and rolled her eyes. She should have guessed Dayana the Fabulous was behind the voices.

"Hmm, no thanks, I've already eaten." Dayana looked over the haul. "Flora, what is all this? I know you packrats are collectors, but this is abnormal. This is hoarding. And now you have the exalted one doing it."

"Excuse me," King Cyrus sniffed. "I'm only assisting so Flora can get home. Flora has a splendid plan, you know." He had no idea what the splendid plan was, of course.

King Cyrus and Dayana looked at Flora, waiting for the plan.

CHAPTER TWENTY-ONE
A SPLENDID PLAN

"**Y**es, I *do* have a plan." Flora was believing she actually had a plan. "Dayana, did you see the owl? Is it still where we left it?" The owl had to be around. They had left it to recover in the clearing past the grove of sagebrush.

"Don't know. I was afraid to go near the place. It must be hungry by now, and I don't want to take any chances."

Just then a humming, stickery mound munched and snuffled his way to the three animals.

"Paco!" Dayana and Flora welcomed their

grown-up porcupine friend.

"Ah, the court jester *and* the court entertainer are here!" King Cyrus stomped his hind foot.

Paco stopped humming and chomping. He waddled toward the spread of luscious twigs and bark. "Mmm." Slobber dribbled from Paco's chattering mouth as he looked over the ready-made feast.

"Not so fast, Paco," said Dayana. "Flora has a splendid plan to get herself home, and for some reason, she needs all this stuff. So you simply need to curb your appetite."

All three animals looked at Flora. A crisp breeze filled her lungs and ruffled her fur.

"Okay, here's the plan." Her friends huddled around as she told them exactly what they need-ed to do.

"But Flora," said Dayana, "this is impossible. I've never heard of such a thing, never. And how will the most important part ever succeed?" She was talking about the owl. The plan couldn't work without him. Paco nodded his head and whapped his tail, planting quills in the ground.

"This calls for a royal decree," King Cyrus said. They all turned and watched him strut back and forth, nose piercing the sky. "Flora has proven herself to be brave and shrewd. The general populace, meaning all those present, will assist with this daring and splendid plan, and they will do so with skill and loyalty."

Flora beamed. Although her plan to get back to the jangly-crate seemed impossible, King Cyrus, Dayana, and Paco would all help her to make it work. Gathering her team of workers, Flora waved her paws and barked orders.

"Alright then, hold on to that bark there, Paco. Dayana, pull that piece this way. Your kinkiness, er, your kindness, King Cyrus, add that twig over there and tie that piece nice and tight. See, you can use that yucca plant fiber. That's it! Don't eat that twig, Paco, can't you wait a little longer? Oh, alright, eat the twig, but keep working. Dayana, you need to untangle your ear from that bunch of bark. That's right, your muskiness, er, your manliness, I mean your mushiness, oh bother, you have to twist that grass just so and pass that piece underneath and over like this, see?" Flora scurried about, directing the placement of every particle until it was perfect.

Determined, they continued working, even as the wind puffed, shaking the leaves of the cottonwood trees. Moving around kept them warm, despite the growing chill. At times the sky flashed in the pitchy darkness.

They all knew when they had satisfied the King's decree and they now crouched around their work. The pieces of canyon debris were no longer scattered willy-nilly. Instead, they had woven and tied together each bark shred, fiber, cactus spine, and twig into a blanket of sorts—a net strong enough to carry a pudgy packrat.

"Paco," said Flora, "I want you to walk into the middle."

Paco waddled onto the blanket and looked at Flora.

"Now, shake, Paco, shake!"

Paco twisted and shivered until a good number of his quills fell.

"That's for added strength," said Flora, "and good luck."

Paco chattered his teeth, raised his nose, and sang out a victory note that joined the rustling leaves and seemed to light up the black night.

But Paco's cry had not lit up the night. Lightning had. A peculiar odor told of coming rain. Lots of it.

Lightning bursts drew closer; Flora's spirits sank. How could the plan succeed now? A heavy storm would ruin everything. And the most important part, the owl, was missing.

But then she felt the saucer eyes behind her.

Her three friends stepped away.

The bird hopped, flexing the wing that had been pierced by Paco's quills. It fixed its gaze on Flora.

Flora knew. Those eyes held her, and she knew. Her plan would work.

Remember, remember, the cliff, the cliff...

"Owl, you know what I need. I know I can count on your help."

In the spitting rain, the owl blinked. At that moment Flora felt big—not pudgy big—but powerful big. Because at that moment she was not just a packrat, separate from an owl, separate from her friends. She was an animal, and they all shared a connection, an understanding they were all in the same animal family. They were all more powerful when they understood that.

That dark empty place in her heart didn't seem so empty. But it was hurting and the lumps were rising. She swallowed hard to force them back down her throat. But they sloshed into her eyes.

"I must leave you now, my friends." Her voice cracked as she turned to them. Whiskers trembled. Three pairs of watery eyes stared at Flora. In a steadier voice, she continued. "I couldn't stop thinking about going home when I got here, but now it's different. Now, I don't want to leave you. You've cared for me and laughed with me and treated me as family."

She turned to Paco and looked at his small eyes peering from his cascade of fur. "Paco, your sweet voice and songs soothed me when I needed it most. And the power you found in your quills saved my life. I will never forget you."

Paco chattered his teeth. "I will m—miss you, Flora." Every one of his quills seemed to shimmer, touching Flora's heart.

She turned to her tall-eared friend. "Dayana, you gave so much in our time together. You shared your joy and your jokes, made me laugh, and taught me the tricks of a ventriloquist. You are a magical and fabulous friend."

Dayana looked at the ground, then at Flora. Her mouth trembled. "You are the magical one, my flabbergasting friend. Because you let me teach you the skills of a ventriloquist, I passed on the craft so important in my family. You have given me a precious gift." Dayana's voice cracked.

Another voice startled Flora. It came from the owl, yet it didn't. "Someday, I want a tail as flea-bitten as yours." Dayana was trying to lighten the mood by poking fun at Flora. But Dayana dissolved into sobs and dabbed her eyes with the tips of her wilted ears.

Flora turned to King Cyrus. Tear trails streaked his grimy face.

"Your most handsome highness, you shared your palace and your knowledge and braved the dangerous unknown for me. You are a magnificent, kind, and just ruler."

King Cyrus puffed up a bit. "Your courage is remarkable, Flora. I will miss you in my palace and kingdom." He sniffed and wrung his floppy front paws.

Flora looked at her friends one last time and stepped onto the blanket they had woven together. She faced the owl, who had watched their goodbyes.

By now the rain was falling steadily and thunder crashed.

The great bird hopped onto the corner of the blanket, nearly brushing Flora's nose. The talons of one foot curled into the blanket. The owl sprang to the other corner on the same side, near the tip of Flora's tail, and curled the talons of its other foot into the blanket. Clutching both corners of one side, the owl jumped over Flora, covering her. She closed her eyes and held her breath. The owl gathered the other side of the blanket in its talons.

Lightning ripped the sky and thunder cracked,

blasting them off the ground.

Flora dangled in the hammock woven of plant scraps and lucky porcupine quills and rose into the swirling darkness.

I'm flying! I'm flying in the air because of this owl. Before, it wanted to eat me—and even now it could rip me up for dinner. Or drop me from the sky. As she rocked and swayed, her nervous thoughts left, and she instead felt snug and secure in the power of the owl.

I'm a pup again! She settled into thoughts of that long-ago time. When she cried for food, her mother nursed her. When she was cold, she snuggled with her brother and sister into the fluff of the nest. When she whimpered, her mother pressed her body next to hers. And now in her flying hammock, feeling as a pup, everything was perfect.

The message came like water singing in a brook, then grew stronger in her thoughts: *Remember the cliff. Home. Remember Flora.*

She rocked to and fro with that gentle message, high above the canyon floor. Every so often they dipped and lurched. The storm beat upon the bird, but its wings seemed strong. Flora stayed dry in her blanket and peered out a small hole amid the bark and twigs.

Her friends had long since disappeared. Rivers of leaves in the canyon bottom turned into the tops of boulders that lit up with the flashing sky. Then the ground seemed dangerously close. They had risen above the canyon walls to the flatter ground on top.

Her heart pounded. She was filled with excitement and dread.

CHAPTER TWENTY-TWO
SOMETHING IMPORTANT

Lightning and thunder turned into a steady rain. The thuds of the raindrops on the soft sand sharpened as they hit the sandstone near the canyon edge. *Ping! Ping! Ping!* The droplets were striking something else. She peered through her sling. A light-colored shape with sharp corners appeared.

The top of the jangly-crate! Smears of light shone out through holes at one end. As they drew closer, her breathing quickened. A loud purring noise shook the air between the raindrops.

She was heavy again, crouching on the ground. The edges of the blanket peeled back like flower petals greeting a new day. Raindrops pelted her nose and she dashed beneath a rabbitbrush.

Her feathered courier stood next to the blanket, flexing its injured wing. Its head appeared flattened and small under its wet feathers.

"Owl," called Flora.

The owl twisted its head and widened its eyes.

Owl, I am so grateful. Flora's heart sent that message. She listened to the yellow saucer eyes.

An honor to serve you, packrat. Remember, remember...

The owl blinked, swiveled its head, and lifted off, trailing its deadly talons. Silently it disappeared.

Most of the clouds had passed. Light drizzle splashed the ground. Tiny streams pushed around Flora. But she focused on something much farther away. In the greyness of that soggy morning, in a clearing at the end of a dirt road, the outline of the jangly-crate appeared.

A rattled hum beckoned. Jitters swept her insides; her feet tingled.

Flora dashed from greasewood bush to sagebrush, through wet sand, around boulders, and over mounded slickrock. Her heart swelled to meet her nest. She could smell it; she could feel it. Sticks and cactus spines, trinkets and treasures, the mirror she found the night she met Grandma Mimi, the twigs she added the night she lost it. The hum grew to a rumble.

"Oh, wait. I'm forgetting something important." She stopped for a few seconds and wrestled in her mind. "I can't go without it. But the jangly-crate might leave any moment. Oh, this won't take long."

She turned and followed her tracks back to the spot where the owl had left her. The blanket lay drenched. Rushing on top, she plucked out the treasure she wanted for her new life.

Now she had to get to the jangly-crate and her nest.

But in the thinning darkness, two bright saucer eyes dazzled her.

The owl had returned. But why? What else did it need to tell her?

She hesitated, then scurried around bushes to get closer. They were not owl eyes. They were the eyes of the jangly-crate.

Flora blinked hard. The rumble deepened and the jangly-crate lurched forward in the chill of the morning, its round feet squishing the soft ground.

"Oh my, no. No, no, you can't go! Wait! Stop!"

Gripping the treasure in her mouth, Flora chased it with all her energy. She needed to jump onto the metal plate underneath while it was moving. But she had to get close enough. She kept running. And the jangly-crate kept escaping.

I can do this, she thought. In the back of her head, Paco, Dayana, and King Cyrus cheered her on. Gertrude and Grandma Mimi called her, urging her forward.

Sputtering and growling, the jangly-crate laid tracks in the dirt. Flora ran, closing the gap between them. *KABOOM!* Foul fumes spewed from its rear, blasting her face. Squinting and spitting, Flora dug her paws into the moist earth, spraying dirt behind her. The roaring noise pushed and blasted, laughing at the desperate packrat.

Run, run. Run faster! Flora panted and ran. *I can make it. Run faster! Faster! Faster...*

It was no use. Flora whimpered and slowed to a stop.

The jangly-crate carrying her nest swayed down the dirt road. It shrank smaller and smaller, then disappeared.

The treasure clutched in her mouth—Paco's good luck quills—dropped silently to the ground.

CHAPTER TWENTY-THREE
ELEGANT TREASURE

Scented sweetness dripped from sagebrush leaves. A pair of tufted titmice birds cheeped and hopped on juniper branches where dots of berries, frosted in sunlight, glowed velvety blue.

The sun's warmth did not reach the forlorn packrat. Stunned and hollow, she peered down that lonely dirt road on that lonely mesa top. Her stark droopy body screamed to flying and skulking predators everywhere, "Get your spicy packrat here—ripe, tender, tasty!" She didn't care, not one bit. It didn't matter.

The jangly-crate had escaped; her life had slipped away. Gone. Poof. Just like that. Her nest couldn't be *gone,* could it? She could still see it in her head. But she clearly wasn't in it.

If only she had not gone back to get the lucky quills. Such a stupid move.

"Let's go back to when I became heavy again, when we landed from the sky," she pleaded to no one and everyone, "and I won't go back for the lucky quills. I won't go back for the lucky quills. I could be in my nest right now, if only...I hadn't gone back."

She moaned and she whimpered and whined and moaned. Who was she, anyway? Flora? Flora the packrat? How about Flora the failure? She reviewed the last few minutes over and over in her head, thinking about what she should have done, instead of what she did.

Her mouth stuck to itself, craving moisture. She nibbled a flattened prickly pear pad, not feeling much at all. Only numbness. Chewing food usually made things better. But that dark place in her heart swelled and didn't even bother to turn into lumps she could push away. The emptiness exploded.

"I'm sorry!" she blurted, her snout and chin slimy with cactus juice. A wail of tears choked her.

She had lost her nest and had let herself and her family of packrats down. It was true—she wasn't sure how—but she knew she had let everyone down. She had made a promise, hadn't she? A promise—to herself, and Grandma Mimi, and the packrats. A promise of some sort, a promise—something she had to do.

For what seemed a long time, she sobbed in despair.

Until an inner voice nudged her from her dark place.

Remember, remember. Flora.

She sniffled. "Alright, I remember. I remember I have friends, right here. I remember how to build a nest. I can build one here. There's plenty to eat, and it's very peaceful, except when there's a thunderstorm."

Remember, Flora, remember.

"I don't want to remember. I don't want to remember how much I want to root through the munch mound with Gertrude and tell stories again with Grandma Mimi."

Remember, remember Flora.

Those words kept nagging her, like a pack of hungry fleas.

"Okay, okay, I remember." She yelled, trying to squelch the inner voice, make it stop, make it go away. "I remember the crack in the cliff, where my ancestors built their home and raised their young. I remember Grandma Mimi's story—an evil beast has claimed that special place. Now no packrat can live there. That's the worst part. Now I'll never be able to go to that place, even if the evil beast has left."

She grew still.

After a while, after her dark thoughts had spoken, her will to move returned. Even though she could not *be* in the old packrat home, she could *remember* it and think about it and all the packrats who had lived there. That helped her to keep going.

Drawing a deep breath, she trudged back toward the precious blanket she and her friends had woven. Along the way, she thought of her nest in the jangly-crate, all the special pieces she had collected—each twig, cactus spine, fleck of paper, metal bit, and shiny discard. Their forms blurred and faded. She sighed. It was time to let it all go, to say goodbye.

Beyond a big yucca, on a smooth rock slab warming in the morning sun, she spied something sparkly—not *small* sparkly, but rather, *big* sparkly.

With her heart aflutter, she waddled past the

yucca's spiked leaves and scrambled onto the slab.

Oh joy, oh joy! Flora hopped and turned circles. A curious collection, slick and metallic shiny, glinted and sparkled in the dawning day. Tiny two-legged creatures were rooted among tiny bloated burrows; miniature jangly-crates with their tiny round feet grew along pathways. Even tinier animals stood frozen in this little world, and near them were small piles of seeds. A crumpled silvery material flowed through the center, curving and twinkling. On its furrowed waves drifted a dimpled vessel, shining like the material beneath it. And separating it all from the outside world was a circle of metal discs with crinkled edges, the same treasures she had collected for her nest. Water droplets shimmered life into every dip, every wrinkle.

"My new nest. This is perfect!" Later she'd figure out where she'd build her nest. For now, collecting lavish decorations seemed most important. She snatched a crinkled disc, then dropped it. Something else lured her—something she could only describe as a doodad—fiery red and no bigger than a mouse. She sniffed and nosed its movable jaw, and examined its strange legs that seemed tied together on each side with a black flexible muscle.

"So elegant, so shiny." She admired the angles, the smooth surface, its odd shape that reminded her of the jangly-crate. Raindrops in its open mouth reflected rainbows. Bold and confident, it seemed ready to roar.

The bright fire of the doodad crackled against the drab color of the sandstone, slamming Flora's senses.

"Yikes! What am I doing out here on this rock? I might as well call the hawks and coyotes for breakfast!" She clamped her mouth around an object, rushed off the rock, and scooted from bush to bush until she reached the woven blanket.

Paco's quills poked through here and there, glinting.

"I can use everything here in my new nest," she announced to no one. As she snuffled over the pile, she imagined how it would look. She'd start with a big prickly pear cactus, and heap twigs and bark and stones and leaves and the blanket itself around the plant, and line a deep cozy spot with juniper bark. And oh, all the discs with the crinkled edges would festoon the walls, and she'd hang shiny crumples above. It would be glorious.

Remember, remember Flora.

She crinkled her nose. There was more to remember?

The ancestral packrat home. Her heart lurched. She yearned for that place. She *belonged* there.

Remember Flora. The words kept tugging on her. There was something else, something about herself?

Just then, the ground shook, lightly at first, tickling Flora's toes.

"What's happening?" Flora darted her eyes and sniffed. The shaking grew stronger, the ground rumbled. She jerked her head, perked her ears, and blinked hard.

From afar crawled a bug. It grew bigger and bigger, louder and noisier, trailing a ribbon of smoke, bobbing, sputtering, popping. *KAPOW!*

"Can it be? Is it? It is! The jangly-crate. My nest. I'm going home? Yes, I'm going home!" For the second time that morning, Flora's heart exploded. But this time, with joy.

Flora didn't think or hesitate for one second. She dashed from rock to greasewood to yucca to sagebrush, stopping at the edge of the clearing where she had first seen the jangly-crate before the sun had risen. Evenly and coolly, she panted. Alert, muscles tensed, ready to unite with her nest.

The jangly-crate stopped and muttered. A

hole opened on the side, and out popped the two-legged pup. His wiry legs ran to the same flat rock she had visited, and he crouched and stuffed the pieces in pockets in his loose skin.

The two-legged pup was the builder of that creation! He seemed to share her love for small and shiny things. She had collected many treasures scattered around the walls of the bloated burrow; he must have brought her those gifts.

"My dozer! My dozer!" His wails pushed Flora into a sprint for the jangly-crate. With pockets bulging, his hands clutched tiny figures as he dashed to and fro on the rock, searching and searching. Face red and twisted, arms raised, something seemed missing from his creation, something precious.

But her eyes did not linger on that scene.

Because in a flash she was snuggled in the fluff and scent of all the perfectly placed sticks, dried cactus pads, ornaments, and shiny things she knew so well. Flora bounced with the rumble of the jangly-crate and stared at the newest treasures she had placed beside her—the shiny red doodad and five of Paco's lucky quills.

CHAPTER TWENTY-FOUR
READY FOR THE WORLD

Pitching in her nest, she slept and woke and saw red, slept and woke and saw red. And always the rumbles—crushing rumbles.

Silence shook her awake. Screechy noises and commotion followed. The jangly-crate rocked and shook. The roof above her nest groaned with thuds and clomps and scrapes. For a long time, she shivered.

A final crash left her nest quivering. Footsteps crunched and melted away. Flora fidgeted her aching body in silence until she moved to the edge of her nest and peeked beyond. In evening's dusky light, she saw a gravel surface—like the gravel strip the jangly-crate had always sat upon.

"Oh my, I'm home. Is it true?" Flora felt a rush of relief, then jumped in the tight space. She needed to be cautious. She waited for the darkness to thicken.

But not for long. Her stomach twisted. She had no fresh prickly pear pads, juniper berries, or green shoots stashed in her nest. With her mouth watering, she lowered herself onto the ground, then crept to the rear of the jangly-crate.

"Is this my home?" She sniffed, crinkling her nose at the lingering smelly fumes. They blotted out the sweet earthiness and prickly pear aromas she knew so well.

Doubts clouded her mind.

"But that *is* the cactus plant I've visited many times." She tried to reassure herself as her hunger gnawed. "But why is it so quiet? I don't hear even a cricket."

She was home, but something was *different*.

"I can't put my paw on it." She searched for movements of predators, sniffed for animal scents, then moved from underneath the jangly-crate and looked up. Wispy clouds wove among themselves in the sparkly sky.

Her stomach rumbled.

"This is ridiculous. It's my home, everything's fine. I need to snibble a snack."

She dashed toward her spiny meal. Arms of linked cactus pads welcomed her. She chomped with gusto, sniffed a noisy breath, and sighed. Home at last. "Oh yum, oh double-yum!" *Smack! Smack!* Her jaws glistened with cactus juice. She paused her blissful chomping, long enough to sense the blanket of quiet, but kept munching.

Then she heard it. A scuffle on the ground nearby. The familiar scent made her heart leap.

"Gertrude! Gertrude!"

"Flora? Is that you?" Her cousin waddled around a chain of cactus pads.

"Flora! Oh, Flora! Where have you been? We thought you had left us, too." The packrat cousins sniffed each other's faces.

"I thought I'd never see *you* again, Gertrude! I'm so happy to be home. You'll never believe where I went and the animals I met and the things I saw and did." Flora launched into her story, spitting pieces of cactus.

"When I couldn't find my nest I thought I was doomed because that place was so different. But I met friends who all wanted to help me get home." She told about each of the animals she met and how she survived all the dangers, rattling on until her mouth ached.

Gertrude did not seem to share in Flora's delight. Although she was listening, her eyes looked dull and distant; her thin body seemed heavy.

Flora watched a tear fall from her cousin's eye and trickle down her nose.

"Gertrude...Gertrude, what is it? Are you alright?"

"It's...it's...my babies...Oh, Flora. I've lost them, every one of them...they're gone!" Gertrude's body shook as she sobbed.

Gone? What did Gertrude mean, *gone*? "What happened? Tell me what happened, Gertrude."

"I went out to eat—the same night you left us—and when I came back, they were gone. Not a hair left! Oh, they weren't ready for the world yet. They needed me for at least ten more days. They weren't ready, they weren't ready..." Gertrude broke down again.

Flora spoke gently to Gertrude. "Maybe they were more ready than you think, Gertrude." But a heavy feeling told her an awful thing had happened. Gertrude's pups needed their mother a little longer before they could strike out on their own.

"No, no. Something got into my nest and

ripped it apart and snatched my babies. I failed them, Flora, I didn't protect them," Gertrude moaned.

A knot grew in Flora's stomach. Gertrude's story sounded all too familiar. Grandma Mimi's story. A mother lost her babies in the old pack-rat home also, to some creature who now claimed that place.

Did the same monster take Gertrude's babies?

"Gertrude, do you know what did this? Did you see the invader? Did it leave any signs? Are you still living in your nest?"

"I saw my nest in shambles, that's all. I was afraid to stay there, but I collected lots of cactus spines to protect it. I might not be safe there, but I guess I don't care."

Gertrude's whiskers trembled. Her body quaked. She darted her eyes past Flora, afraid she would meet at any moment the villain who stole her babies.

"You can stay with me in my nest, Gertrude, in the jangly-crate." What a surprising offer. Flora had never shared her nest, as packrats don't do that, other than with their young.

Gertrude cocked her head, then sighed. "Thanks, Flora, but I think I'll be alright. Besides, Grandma Mimi told me I needed to stay in my nest and fortify it even more with twigs and the thorniest cactus pads I could find."

"You met Grandma Mimi?"

"Yes, I found her on the flat place attached to the bloated burrow the next night. I don't go there ever, but I was looking for my babies and there she was. I told her what happened. She listened and even cried with me and gave me some comfort."

"Did she talk about anything else? Did she talk about the cliff?"

Gertrude's mouth dropped. "Flora, why would she talk about that awful place? Remember, we're supposed to beware of the dreaded cliff." She looked closely at Flora.

"Oh, I thought maybe..." Flora did not want to frighten Gertrude even more by telling her about the packrat home where a monster with a history of eating baby packrats lived. "You're right, Gertrude. Grandma Mimi is comforting and wise."

"She seemed to understand exactly how I felt." Talking about Grandma Mimi seemed to calm the cousins.

"When I told her you and the jangly-crate were gone, she was worried."

"Oh my, I must find her so she knows I'm alright."

"She'll be so relieved to see you, Flora." Gertrude dribbled tears again. "At least you came back, Flora. I wish my babies were back, too."

Flora looked at Gertrude, wrenched in pain from her loss. Flora felt it was her loss, too.

"Gertrude, I'll help you carry some cactus pads to your nest in the woodpile. Then I must search for Grandma Mimi."

They gnawed off several pads and crammed them in their mouths. As they dashed from one bush to the next, they watched the shadows for movements and listened for strange sounds. There was nothing but an eerie quiet. Both were panting when they reached the woodpile.

"Gertrude, I'll leave these here. See you later at the prickly pear cactus?"

"I don't want to be out any longer, Flora. Maybe tomorrow night." Gertrude disappeared into the woodpile, carrying a spiny pad. Her head popped out.

"Remember the cliff, Flora. Beware of the cliff. Don't go near the dreaded cliff."

CHAPTER TWENTY-FIVE
HELPLESS

The cliff was not where Flora was headed. Focused on a mission, she scurried to the wall of the bloated burrow and followed it to the corner where the big barrel collected water. Grandma Mimi had sent her to this place the night they met. She had found the shiny mirror here. It was in her nest somewhere. But now she had other things to think about as she headed for the steps.

She could not avoid it. The dreaded cliff. Catching a glimpse, she felt a pang, jagged, like the dark crack scoring its face. She tried to shake the feeling as she climbed, hoping to find Grandma Mimi.

Ah, eggplants. Purple bulbs glinted in the light shining through the holes of the bloated burrow. But no Grandma Mimi. *Patience, Flora. Grandma Mimi will come.*

The aroma pulled Flora's plumpness into the box. With eyes half closed, she slid her teeth down the squeaky skin. "So subliminal, so subliming." She wasn't sure about the words, but they sounded good. For extra oomph, she moaned a mash-up word, saved for the absolute best of food heaven treats. "Sublorious!" So clever, two words in one: "sublime" and "glorious." She ripped the chewy flesh. *Smack, shlosh!*

Wait, wait. She shook her head. There was another reason why she was there. Flora perked her ears and sniffed the air for Grandma Mimi. "Where is she? She loves eggplants. I'll wait a little longer."

She crammed a few leaves in her mouth, plopped down from the box, and crept to the top of the steps. Shivering in the silence, she inflated her lungs and looked at the cliff.

Its curves and angles reflected light from a partial moon. The jagged crack, so dark, pulled on her. Even though she was sitting, she felt as if she were traveling into that crack. Twisting tunnels and dark rooms and mysteries and secrets and stories wrapped around her.

She wasn't scared, because a cluster of small paws walked with her, keeping her company. It felt so old, this place. Her fur brushed the rocks and dirt and sticks. She belonged here.

"Flora!" They called her. "Flora!"

The creaky voice made her jerk and feel the hard wood surface. "Flora! Is that you?"

"Grandma Mimi?" Dazed, Flora plunked down the steps. "Oh, Grandma Mimi, it's you, it's you!" She hopped and thumped her hind leg.

"Hello, young one. I thought I smelled a pack-rat up there." Grandma Mimi's clouded eyes widened. "I'm so glad to find you. I was worried you were gone for good."

"I've seen the world, Grandma Mimi, I've *lived* in another world." Flora pranced in circles. When she calmed down, she announced, "But I am back now, here to stay." Her experiences with King Cyrus, Paco, and Dayana came to life in a tumble of words. Grandma Mimi grunted now and then as Flora relived her adventures. When she talked about the owl, the old packrat moved her tattered ears.

"The owl *talked* to me, Grandma Mimi. It was so strange because everyone knows owls can't talk. I was the only one who could hear it. Its eyes were so spooky, like they could see into me."

"What did the owl say, Flora?"

Flora grew still, recalling those yellow saucers. "It said things like, '*We are one*' and '*Know your strength*.' Was it talking about me, Grandma Mimi? And it said, '*You shall find your home. Remember.*' But I'm not sure what it wanted me to remember."

"And what else, Flora, what else did it say?"

"The owl said, '*Remember, remember the... cliff*.'" Flora shook her head. "Or was that in my dream? How could that owl know about the cliff?"

She looked at Grandma Mimi for answers. A tear was dripping from the corner of her eye. Grandma Mimi could barely see. Gray hairs glinted on her scarred muzzle. She wheezed and gurgled, something Flora had not noticed when they last met

Grandma Mimi is dying. Flora's throat tightened. *She's dying.* This truth stared at her, sank into her heart, and wouldn't leave. She couldn't do anything. Just feel it and know it, as she was doing with the darkness of the night surrounding them at that moment.

Grandma Mimi seemed to hear her thoughts. She closed her tired eyes. "Flora, I want to tell you something I didn't tell you earlier. It's about our family home and what happened."

A dullness was creeping over Flora, stealing the happiness she had felt from talking with Grandma Mimi again. Something was coming from the old one, something important. And sad. She didn't want to know it. But she moved closer.

"Remember the creature," Grandma Mimi winced, dropping her voice to a whisper, "that took the babies of the mother packrat who lived there?"

"Yes, so terrible, he took them while the mother was out searching for food, and she never...she never saw..." Flora's eyes grew wide. "Oh, Grandma Mimi! They were *your* babies, weren't they?"

Grandma Mimi's eyes welled up with tears. "I couldn't save them, I couldn't do anything. I felt so...so...*helpless*. I was too afraid to go back, and I never found out what killed my babies. And now it's happened again...to Gertrude's babies."

"The same beast...the same one, I'm sure of it. It took babies from you and Gertrude. It had no right to be there. Our ancestors—our grandmothers and great-grandmothers and their pups had been there all along—it was their place, *our* place, the great packrat birthplace, and that beast took it from all the packrat mothers who ever lived there, and who were *meant* to live there."

Flora's tiny nostrils flared. Her eyes narrowed. When the fumes of her anger cleared, she sat there, feeling those old lumps from the deep rising from that dark lonely place in her heart. They softened and spilled into warm tears, washing that place in her heart, cleaning off more lumps so they could rise and spill, rise and spill.

CHAPTER TWENTY-SIX
DESTINY

Messages smoldered in Flora, like hot coals refusing to burst into flames. Dark. Cloudy. Where were the messages from? The owl? Her dreams? Or was she making them up? They confused her; she didn't want them. But she couldn't smother them, so she had to listen and understand.

You know more than you know. Brave packrat. My home, home. Remember the cliff. Ancestral home. My home. We are one. You know. Brave packrat. Remember Flora.

The words churned until she stopped trying to understand them. Closing her eyes, she remembered when she felt the owl's gratitude after removing the quills. That same feeling filled her heart again, and she felt big. There was nothing to say or do. She was there, sitting with the gratitude in her heart and the words, letting them burn.

The words sharpened. Confidence puffed her face, lengthened her body, and rippled her fur. Now she knew.

"Grandma Mimi, there's something I must do." Although the message was clear inside her, it was having a hard time getting out, out past the shadows.

"What is it, young one?"

"I must take back our ancestral home." Her faint words floated, nearly melting away, as if she was trying on the idea, seeing if it was solid, real.

But she firmed her jaw and raised her head. Facing the dreaded cliff, she called out, "I am taking back our ancestral home." Her words bounced off the cliff and shimmied her ears.

This was her destiny. She had no doubt.

She turned to Grandma Mimi. Sadness faded to joy in the old packrat's face.

"Flora, you are a special packrat. I am so proud to know you."

Her words were like liquid sunshine wrapped in the plumpest, most mouthwatering prickly pear pad.

Flora and Grandma Mimi turned their noses toward the dreaded cliff with the crack sheltering the great packrat birthplace, their ancestral home.

CHAPTER TWENTY-SEVEN
CLUES

"I need to get closer," she had told Grandma Mimi. "So I can find out what beast has taken over our old packrat home. I'll search for clues."

Now she was in a totally new place, a jangly-crate distance away from the dreaded cliff. It seemed monstrous hanging over her. A jumble of boulders grew from the ground, creating pockets and cracks and overhangs where she could creep unseen. She crouched under a skunkbush, heart throbbing, trying not to blink. The dark crack stretched from the ground to high in the cliff face.

A movement. No sound, but something stirred low in the crack.

What is it? Sticks in the packrat home, a lizard, an insect? Wisps of a spider's trail? I must have blinked. It's a dark hole with nothing there.

Squinting, she tried to steady her trembling and pick out a form, a shape. She listened for footsteps, the crunch of dried leaves, the panting of a hungry predator, the hiss of a beast on the run.

Squeezing her mind hard, she felt herself leaving her body. A mixture of odors from decaying plants, moist earth, crushed sagebrush leaves, fading rabbitbrush blossoms, and animal urine took over her thoughts.

Off the ground she floated, drifting toward the crack.

Leaves rustled, branches scratched, jarring her. She zipped back to her shivering body under the skunkbush, shaking her head and gulping air.

"I've got to pull myself together. Something might see me, chase me. I need to be able to run... Oh no, can it see my eyes? They can always see the eyes."

The twigs of the packrat home twisted and shook. Again, sticks shifted and scraped. She blinked. A flash, a gliding shadow, a faint rustle. Eerie silence.

A chill sickened her stomach. She didn't move. She couldn't move.

She was petrified.

It can hear me. It can see me. She wanted to moan, wail, release her utter terror. Panting. Panting. Loud panting.

Pull yourself together, Flora!

Sounds crept into her head. Paco's lullaby—the one he had sung to the owl stricken by his quills—washed her icy limbs with calm.

Warming her stiff lungs, she planned her next step. Whatever was in the crack could be watching her, waiting for her to make a careless move. But the crack was still some distance away.

She searched for clues. *Maybe the beast left some fur or feathers on the plants near the crack. Hmm, nothing. Not even any droppings. How will I figure out what this creature is?*

Flora looked at the ground where she had pressed her trembling paws. She felt the nose of King Cyrus prodding her. *Tracks—I'll look for tracks.*

Slender trunks of Gambel oak trees lined the cliff base. Between the oak trunks and the sandstone wall was a narrow pathway of sand—particles of the cliff that had crumbled.

I'll find tracks there—right next to the cliff wall,

under the trees.

She moved beneath bushes and squeezed through tunnels under rock slabs. The cliff wall was a tail's length away.

Watching the crack, she scanned the sand at her feet. A sprinkling of cone-shaped pits dimpled the surface.

Ah, ant snatchers. Flora thought back to when she was a curious youngster. She had dropped an ant on the sloped side of a similar pit near the wall of the bloated burrow. The ant rolled. Tiny claws of the ant snatcher, buried at the bottom, darted out in a flurry of flying sand. It snatched the ant right before her horror-stricken eyes.

For an instant, she pictured a swarm of fierce ant snatcher claws thrashing around the old pack-rat nest in the crack.

"That's ridiculous. Ant snatchers have not taken over our ancestral home." She left the ant snatcher traps and their buried builders in peace.

Instead, she examined the crisscross pattern of long thin trails connecting pit to pit. Then she noticed it. The delicate trails of the ant snatchers were broken by another mark. A scatter of small footprints. Just a mouse. Something else. A long, smooth furrow meandered through the sand, like an old, lazy river. The sides of the furrow rose and fell in waves. Flora crinkled her nose. As she grew numb, the awful truth seeped in.

"Oh my. My tail...but it's not my tail." It wasn't the shallow groove left by a tail dragged between animal feet. It was the deeper, broader mark of a creature with *no* feet.

Only one animal could leave such a mark.

Snake.

Her mind filled that channel with the body of a snake, a big one, bigger than she had ever imagined. She shuddered. In her mind's eye, she could see neither the head nor tail because it was super long.

Her eyes followed the swale as it pressed the sand along the cliff, slithered around an oak trunk, and sank deeper. Then stopped.

"Oh no," she whispered. Her discovery couldn't get any worse, but it did. Searching, she found no sign the snake had kept going. Right above where the tracks ended, Flora's gaze melted into the crack in the cliff. Its darkness was stuffed with the memories of her ancestors.

CHAPTER TWENTY-EIGHT
BUBBA

Flora scampered from the cliff back to the steps. Grandma Mimi was waiting underneath a rabbitbrush.

"It's awful, Grandma Mimi." Choking for air, her stomach galloped and her legs shook. A breeze crinkled the cottonwood leaves and ruffled Flora's fur, chilling her.

"What did you find, Flora?"

"Snake," she panted. "I'm sure. A *big* snake. Its tracks went right to the crack."

Grandma Mimi closed her eyes and tightened

her face. "Oh, Flora, that is serious. It all makes sense now..."

"Grandma Mimi, I've never met a snake and I don't want to. My mother warned me about these creatures that can get into our nests if we don't protect them enough...and they squeeze animals to death before they eat them. And sometimes they don't even squeeze them first. Sometimes their bite has *venom*." Flora's trembling voice rose.

"Yes, Flora, different kinds of snakes hunt our kin. Some do things you wouldn't imagine—crawl into animal burrows, climb trees, and even swim. They love to eat small animals like us, especially... especially babies."

Flora moaned. "How am I ever going to take back our home from an animal like that?"

"I don't know, Flora." Her eyes closed as she shook her head and whispered. "I don't know."

Flora kept looking at Grandma Mimi for an answer. A snake—a monstrous snake, a killer snake, a snake with no end, a snake that could climb trees and swim and slither past cactus spines in a packrat nest—this creature was no match for a rotund packrat like herself. Grandma Mimi had all the answers, she had to tell her what to do. But her frayed whiskers moved not a twitch.

Flora calmed her thoughts and closed her

eyes, searching inside herself for an answer. She heard it, although it made little sense at first.

Bubba.

"Huh? *Bubba?*" What a strange word. Flora rolled her eyes. "Bubba. Is this a joke?" Dayana was grinning with ears crossed inside Flora's head, clear as a prickly pear pad. That rabbit could hurl insults and say the silliest things, making even the scariest situations kind of funny.

"Alright then. I'll call the snake Bubba." Flora's ears perked up. "It must have bubbles on its butt. And boogers up its nose. Jeez, Flora, you're so clever." She giggled.

Grandma Mimi's mouth dropped open. "Are you alright, dearie? What's happened? Did you say boogers? Bubbles? *Bubba butt?*"

"I'm okay. It was Dayana, my friend. She helped me calm down. She helped me get another view."

Grandma Mimi seemed puzzled but relieved.

Flora felt a little stronger. "Grandma Mimi, I need to know more about snakes. Do you think Bubba snake saw me tonight? It didn't come after me."

"Maybe he wasn't hungry, Flora. I don't think snakes eat every day."

"How thick is their fur? Bubba didn't leave any near the crack."

"Ahh, now this is something I do know." Grandma Mimi closed her eyes, searching her memory. "Snakes don't have fur. They have smooth skin they crawl out of when they get tired of it. When I was young, I saw a snake's skin hanging on a bush. I could almost see right through it. It looked like it was staring back at me because it still had eye skin." She shuddered. "Like a scary ghost."

Yikes. What's worse, facing Bubba the ghost or Bubba the snake? Flora didn't want to find out. For now, she needed to know more about Bubba the snake.

"No fur? How do they keep warm? And how come I've never met one?" The breeze had gotten stronger. Flora leaned closer to Grandma Mimi to hear.

"I've seen only one. When I was young, I wandered outside our home near the craggy juniper tree. The sun was rising, and the light got in my eyes. I crawled over some sticks. One of the sticks moved." Grandma Mimi winced. "It was a snake."

Flora's eyes widened. "Oh, Grandma Mimi, you were almost killed!"

"But I felt no danger. It hardly moved. I think it was sleeping. It felt like a cold stick, but kind of squishy. My mother was angry. She said if it had been later in the day I would have been a snake snack."

"Later in the day?"

"I'm not sure why she said that. But she told me to never go out in the daylight again and to fetch food at night, so I could hide better." Grandma Mimi looked thoughtful. "Maybe that snake wanted to show off its skin in the sunshine."

"Hmm, interesting. A vain snake, a show-off. A cold animal that can peel off its skin when it gets tired of it. What an odd creature."

An odd creature that had a taste for young packrats.

CHAPTER TWENTY-NINE
HEAVY WORRIES

Gusty winds flapped Flora's ears. The clouds had thickened, drowning the wash of stars from much earlier. Darkness would soon grow thin. She needed to leave Grandma Mimi and return to her nest.

Flora wore a sack of worries. The heaviest: how to conquer a snake. This task seemed as big as the canyon walls in the world she had left. A snake was big, eye-popping big. A snake could hide from her, bite her, eat her. It was a strange shape. No legs.

Was a snake clever? Unknown.

But a snake *was* probably ugly.

She had found a way to rise above the canyon walls in the other place. She had to remember that. And she had faced another animal that could have eaten her: Owl.

As she heard Grandma Mimi puffing, she knew one thing for sure. She must find a way to take back the old packrat home.

"Grandma Mimi, I know there is a way to get our home back. I need a plan." She tried to sound confident for Grandma Mimi. But mostly, for herself.

The old packrat's eyes drifted. Flora strained to hear her. "Our home—remember—find our home." Her words trailed off as she snoozed.

Flora tried to ignore Grandma Mimi's gurgling, her stiff paws, the bald spots in her scruffy fur. Grandma Mimi felt like the packrat family Flora yearned to have in her life. Forever. But Grandma Mimi would leave her. The dark deep in her heart tried to push out some lumps, but she held them there and thought about something else.

Way back in the web of thoughts in Flora's mind, she saw the mother of all packrats, the Super Mama. The biggest, oldest mother packrat ever. The Super Mama looked like Grandma Mimi, and she spilled the motherly love Flora craved. Warm gooey love. That's all Flora felt for a moment and she relaxed.

She whispered goodnight to Grandma Mimi, and ran around the bloated burrow past Gertrude's woodpile, across the ditch. Snatching a bite of prickly pear pad, she snapped off some spines. "That snake can never find my nest. Never!" Until now she had not doubted its safety.

Her thoughts raced as she jumped into her nest and placed the fresh cactus spines.

She had to find the way. She had to make a plan.

Her trinkets stared at her. She stared back. Everything was in order—perfect, predictable, just as she liked.

The plan—the plan to take back the ancestral packrat home—needed a lot of thought. Especially since at the moment, Flora had no idea what it looked like.

CHAPTER THIRTY
A FEW HOLES

Flora somersaulted through her dreams. Her treasures floated around and spiraled down a hole. Baby packrats cried. Notes from Paco's lulla-by danced. King Cyrus' nose pointed at her and he cried, "You befuddled packrat!" Leaves and rocks and prickly pear pads and tree trunks all sprang to life and traded insults. Dayana looked on with her ears crossed, laughing.

A shadow invaded her dreamscape. Smooth and thick, she couldn't see the edges. It moved but stayed the same. In her dream Flora felt a sharp pain in her neck, cold squeezing her butterball body. Her eyes bulged; she couldn't breathe. Everything went black.

She jerked awake.

"Am I safe?" she said aloud.

"You are safe. You know what to do."

Did someone speak? Or did I think that? No response.

Flora inflated her chest and blew. She cuddled in her fur coat, rubbing against all her treasures, grabbing a moment of peace. Troubling dreams, but she felt calm and refreshed.

"Hey—what? Oh my, I think I have a plan." Flora twitched her toes. "Oh my, oh my, I *do* have a plan!"

Her dueling voice—the one she knew well from the past, croaked in the back of her head.

There are a few holes—but it is a plan.

CHAPTER THIRTY-ONE
OMEN

Flora moved briskly. She might not have enough time to get all the pieces in place for her plan to work. There were so many treasures to gather from her nest and carry to the other side of the bloated burrow. That was the first part of the plan.

But she needed to eat.

The winds had brought frosty coolness. Flora shivered as her toes hit the cold earth. Gertrude was already at the prickly pear cactus.

"Flora!" Gertrude was happy to see her cousin.

"Gertrude!" Flora dropped her bundle next to

the cactus and bit into a fleshy pad.

"Why are you carrying those...things? Those aren't cactus spines. What are they?"

"They're going to help me with my plan. Something for good luck." Flora beamed.

Gertrude eyed her cousin. "What plan? What are you doing, Flora? We all need good luck, but those should be in your nest to protect it. And why do you have that...that look about you?" Gertrude darted her eyes at Flora, beyond her, behind her.

Flora twitched her whiskers.

"Gertrude, I must do something. For you and for all of us. I want you to feel safe—and not worry that the monster that took your babies is going to return."

"But Flora, don't be silly; there's no way you can stop that beast." Gertrude's voice turned to a whisper. "You don't even know what it is."

"But I do know what the beast is. I have a plan. I know what I must do." Gertrude stopped munching and looked wide-eyed at Flora.

"It's a snake. I saw his tracks. He lives in the crack in the cliff."

"Oh, Flora. The *dreaded* cliff? A *snake*? You're crazy, Flora. No, no! You can't go near that place. You mustn't!"

"I have to, Gertrude." She softened her voice.

"I'll have lots of help, too."

Gertrude stared at Flora.

"A snake..." Gertrude moaned and shook her head. "I should have known. My mother always told me a snake could go almost anywhere, even into our nests. You need to use lots of cactus pieces to protect your nest, she said."

"Oh, Gertrude. You did your best with your nest; I know you did."

"But I should have listened to her better. She told me to be extra careful when the days are hot, and the nights still warm, because the snake becomes a night stalker. That's when I lost them."

Flora felt Gertrude's regret. But there was something Gertrude said: "*When the days are hot, and the nights still warm, the snake becomes a night stalker.*"

One of the holes in her plan just filled up. Until then, Flora was not sure when the snake would move around—day or night. Gertrude had helped answer that question, refining her plan. *Although there might be a couple of teeny tiny more holes.*

"Will you help me, Gertrude?"

"What do you want? I don't want to go near the dreaded cliff, and I can't face a snake—especially the one who...who...took my babies."

"Only do what you feel comfortable doing. For

now, I need you to carry a few of my treasures to the other side of the bloated burrow."

Gertrude twitched her whiskers. She looked at the ground for a moment and faced Flora. "Alright." Her small voice betrayed her fear. But Flora knew she could count on Gertrude.

The two friends locked eyes for a moment, chewed the cactus pads, and swallowed.

"Follow me!" Off they scuttled to the jangly-crate, Flora in the lead.

Deep in her nest, Flora dug through her hoard. She muttered and complained and stopped now and then to admire a treasure. "Now where did I put that thing? Oh, there it is. Wow, I don't remember this...Look at the twinkles on this doohickey. Where'd I get that? Goodness, Flora, focus. You don't need *all* this stuff."

Out of her nest, she pitched flashy baubles and thingamabobs, gizmos and keepsakes, and odd-shaped rocks and sticks.

"Flora, what are you doing?" Gertrude whisper-yelled as the pile grew.

"Wait a sec, Gertrude. Can't forget these." Cactus spines rained on Gertrude's nose.

"You could have warned me!"

Flora emerged with more loot. "Here, carry these. Oh, and this little gem, too. One more thing." She shoveled the things into Gertrude's mouth and paws.

"I can't carry any more, Flora."

"Okay, we'll come back. Now follow me." Flora grabbed the good luck items she had first removed.

Around the walls of the bloated burrow, they scurried to the bottom of the steps, where they dumped their loads.

"Grandma Mimi is not here, but I'm sure she'll come. I talked with her last night," said Flora. Turning her head, she noticed a form drifting toward them from the shadows. "Here she comes now."

The old packrat limped, stopping every few steps to sniff the ground. Her eyes were nearly useless. She had to rely instead on her sense of smell.

Flora heard her wheezing long before she reached the two cousins. "Grandma Mimi, it's me and Gertrude. We're here."

Grandma Mimi dragged her bulk faster until she found them. "I thought...I smelled both of you. I was...out for food. I was hoping...a morsel from up there had...fallen." Grandma Mimi could barely talk, much less climb the steps to the eggplants.

"I'll go get one for you." Flora dashed up the

steps, climbed on the box with eggplants, and snipped off a vegetable. She bit into another and nearly swooned.

"Mmm. Heavenly." Pieces flew from her mouth. She relaxed into munching. Her eyes drifted to the cliff.

There it was. The crack, the dark crack, with the old packrat home. *Oh my, did those sticks twitch?* Flora's heart pounded. *Are packrat ghosts in there, having fun? Oh please, couldn't that be what's in there, please?* Her chewing slowed, then stopped. Knots grew in her stomach. The crunched-up mess fell from her mouth. She was not hungry.

"What am I doing? What am I *doing*? I'm avoiding what I need to do." She looked deeper into the crack. "He's in there. He's in there, and he shouldn't be there. He's in my ancestral home. He's taken over *our* home."

Images flashed: baby packrats getting grabbed, squeezed, swallowed whole. *Squeezed to death by a snake.*

"Ohh!" she cried, remembering her dream. "My dream was an omen. I'm going to die trying to take back the old packrat home." Her voice was cold, flat.

Night noises grew louder. Gertrude and Grandma Mimi called her.

"I'm coming!" She grew determined. More than determined. Jaw firm, her thoughts cleared.

"I know what I must do. I may die. But *I'm* making that choice. No one is forcing me. Like when I crawled under the wing of that owl while my friends howled at me." She smiled a little, remembering how her action led to the owl helping her find her nest. "This is almost the same."

Steadying her gaze into the crack, she added, "Except the stakes are higher. Much higher."

Flora had a plan to take back the ancestral packrat home. It was time to make Flora's plan work.

CHAPTER THIRTY-TWO
REMEMBERING WHO I AM

Grandma Mimi sniffed the eggplant Flora brought her, then chomped with gusto. Despite her problems, her appetite was strong.

"Flora, I thought you had a plan," said Gertrude.

"I do have a plan. Help me carry the rest of my supplies."

The cousins scurried to the pile of treasures beneath the jangly-crate They crammed their mouths, ran to the steps and dumped their load, then hurried back. Back and forth they traveled until they had moved most of the pile thrown from Flora's nest.

"There!" said Flora. "We can rest before the next step."

"Next step?" Gertrude panted and paced.

"That was the first step. We have a long night ahead of us, Gertrude." Gertrude's eyes widened. She looked to Grandma Mimi, dozing nearby, to see what she thought of all the activity.

"Find a way, Flora," Grandma Mimi murmured, barely cracking her eyes open.

Flora felt a pang. Grandma Mimi's voice sounded weak, distant.

"I'm going to make my plan work." *Even if there are a few teeny-weeny holes.* She looked at Grandma Mimi's face. Her heart pleaded, *please stay with us, Grandma Mimi.*

Flora and Gertrude munched on rabbitbrush twigs while they examined the pile. It was bigger than the two of them.

"Where is that crazy quilt? Oh, there it is. And the cactus bits, and that shiny thingy, and that doo-dad, the good luck spikeys, yep, they're all here." No matter she wouldn't use most of the hoard for her plan. Just *moving* her treasures closer to the old packrat home seemed important. The proper packrat thing to do.

"Flora, I don't understand the next step. Most of your nest is sitting right here in this pile. It doesn't make any sense."

"Here's where it gets hard. I'll tell you what I need. You don't have to help, but the plan will go a lot faster if you do."

Gertrude's face looked stricken when Flora asked her to carry a few things closer to the dreaded cliff.

"I told you I don't want to go near that place. It's forbidden! And if that killer monster lives there...no, it's too dangerous."

"But I went there last night, Gertrude, and nothing bad happened to me." That was far from true. The place had nearly sent Flora into a stupor of terror. "We'll go a teensy bit closer, Gertrude. We'll be very watchful." Flora paused. "Just one trip. Then we'll return and you can be with Grandma Mimi."

They both looked at Grandma Mimi wheezing with her eyes closed.

"Besides, the snake will not be a danger to us. You told me so yourself."

"What do you mean? I didn't say that."

"But you said, 'When the days are hot, and the nights still warm, the snake becomes a night stalker.' Gertrude, the day was not hot, and this night is cold, therefore, that beast will NOT stalk us tonight." Flora beamed.

"Ohh. Wait...you're saying because the night is cold, that fiend won't eat us?"

"Well, kind of. It's all logical. I'm certain I saw the snake in the crack last night. But it's much colder tonight than last night. He'd rather hole up until it is warmer during the day. He has no fur, and he gets cold if the air is cold, and he acts like a slug, or a big stick."

Gertrude's confused face lit up. "So, snakes are like packrats—they don't like to move around on hot days, and instead move around at night when it's cool. But when it's too cold at night, they'd rather be out during—"

"And besides, his name is Bubba, and he has boogers on his butt and bubbles in his nose. Or maybe boils on his bottom."

Gertrude stared at Flora. "Have you gone *mad*?"

"Lightening the mood, Gertrude. So, we can get a different view—make things less scary."

Gertrude's jaw dropped. The Bubba-bubbles-butt-booger thing didn't seem to be lightening Gertrude's mood. She rolled her eyes. Moaned. Faked a laugh. "Well, how are you going to deal with this monster? He won't be wandering around until it gets warm, and you'll be back in your nest—what's left of it. He'll go looking for you. And *me*."

"He won't ever know you were near the cliff, Gertrude." In truth, Flora wasn't so sure about that. "Don't worry, you won't be in danger. You're probably right, he'll be looking for me, but it's all part of the plan."

Gertrude's eyes widened. "Flora, you're a packrat, remember? If that brute sees you, he'll want to eat you. He ate my babies. How can you defeat a snake? You've forgotten who you are, Flora."

Was Gertrude right? *Have I forgotten who I am?* Flora's adventures told her something else. She had traveled to another world and back, befriended strangers, survived predators, talked with an owl, flown through the air, and had a plan to meet a snake. Would she take back the old packrat home? Maybe, maybe not. Maybe she'd die. But the word-loving, prickly-pear-cactus-eating packrat goddess was someone different now, yet someone she'd been all along. She kind of liked that someone different.

Flora raised her head and pulled big air into her packrat lungs.

"No, Gertrude, that's just it. I haven't forgotten

who I am—I am *remembering* who I am."

A halo of sparks seemed to crackle around Flora, throwing prickles on Gertrude's nose and in her ears. Nearby, Grandma Mimi shifted as she spluttered and muttered something. Flora thought she heard the word "remember."

"Now, will you help me, Gertrude? The second step of the plan needs to begin."

Gertrude firmed her jaw. "Only one trip, then I'm going to sit with Grandma Mimi."

"Oh, Gertrude, you're so brave."

Flora dug through the pile. She pulled out a few items and stuffed them into Gertrude's mouth, muffling her protests.

"You can do it, Gertrude." Flora grabbed the most precious item of all, the smooth mirror she had found behind the water barrel the night she met Grandma Mimi. It kept slipping from her mouth, but she felt powerful as she carried this special gift.

The packrats picked their way through the greasewood and sagebrush toward the dreaded cliff. Flora scampered ahead of Gertrude, urging her on. Before they reached the boulders, they dropped their burdens.

"See, it's not so scary, is it Gertrude?" Flora whispered.

"Uh." Gertrude grunted, backed up, and led the dash back.

By the time they returned to the pile at the steps, Grandma Mimi was asleep and sputtering.

"I'm done, Flora," Gertrude panted, still shaking. "I'll sit with Grandma Mimi now. What's wrong with her, Flora? She's fast asleep and making those...noises."

"Grandma Mimi." Flora nudged her gently, lowering her voice.

The old packrat stirred and moved her mouth. Her eyes were closed. "Flora...home...home," she murmured.

Flora's throat tightened. "It won't be long now." She could barely hold back her tears as she whispered in Grandma Mimi's ear. "I know the way to take back our ancestral home."

Grandma Mimi sighed, falling into a relaxed sleep.

Flora and Gertrude exchanged a troubled look. But there was no time to linger over Grandma Mimi. The night was wearing on. Flora's plan had to be in place before sunrise.

"Gertrude, now I will leave you both. The third step of the plan needs to begin." Flora's voice grew somber. "Whatever happens, do not go near the cliff while I'm gone. I won't see you again this evening, but I'll look for you here tomorrow night. If I'm not here, well…do not go near the cliff, ever."

Flora locked eyes with her cousin and lifelong friend. They both shared thoughts of their munch mound searches and chomping prickly pear cactus together. Gertrude's eyes welled up with tears and her whiskers quivered. Flora blinked and dropped her gaze. "Gertrude—my forever cousin-friend."

She turned to the grey whiskers, torn ears, and billowing folds of Grandma Mimi. Her wrinkled face looked peaceful, lost in a deep sleep. Flora thought of their first meeting when she learned the truth about the dreaded cliff and the ancestral packrat home in the crack. Grandma Mimi longed to go back. Now Flora shared that yearning. Both were destined to return; Flora was certain. But Grandma Mimi seemed so weak. Pain thumped at Flora's heart. She shoved it away. She needed to get going.

"Thank you, Grandma Mimi. I won't let you down."

CHAPTER THIRTY-THREE
SETTING THE TRAP

Flora pulled a tangled bundle—the crazy quilt—from the pile. Its texture had attracted her weeks ago when she found it on the ground near the berry patch. Tough threads wove themselves in small squares. Tight little knots dotted the places where the threads crossed. All sorts of twigs and leaves and papery fragments clung to it, like a spider's web. *Jackpot!* she thought as she dragged it to her nest that night.

This wad was the key.

Now it spilled from her mouth like a foamy

mustache as she carried it to the cliff. Gertrude's voice floated after her. "You can do it, Flora! You can do it, my friend!"

Boulders rose around her as she ferried all the trinkets even closer to the cliff. She rested in her hiding spot from the previous night, her breath condensing in misty clouds. Cozy in her coat of warm fur, calm and confident, Flora spied the dark crack.

"Bubba. The furless monster is in there. He's probably cold and miserable in my home. He has no idea what's coming. Get to work, Flora."

The third step of the plan began with a flurry of packrat mutterings.

"Those tree trunks are perfect. No, maybe I should use that one and that one; yes that's good. How can I straighten out this crazy quilt? It's all snarled! Snarled...snarled...I like that word. Oh my...Don't unravel the thing, Flora. Oh, that's the problem, all these twigs and juniper shreds and leaves need to come out. If I could get this part stretched up that tree."

She tugged and wrestled that crazy quilt until it was smoothed out and nearly perfect. Every few minutes she stopped, admired her progress, glanced at the dark crack, and looked up the cliff wall and around the boulders, reassuring herself she was safe.

Flora untwisted the wad into the thin, nearly invisible net she had found near the berry patch. She stepped back and sucked in air.

"Oh, this is fantastic. It's going to work, it's going to work!"

The net stretched among several trees that bordered the cliff wall. She had removed the bits of junk that clung to its strands. Cactus spines pinned its sides around the tree trunks and its bottom flush to the ground. Flora studied the crack beyond but barely saw the net in between. Perfect!

She grabbed several of Paco's quills from her pile of loot and jabbed those slender spears into the ground near the net. They weren't just for good luck. Paco's quills had crippled a powerful owl. She remembered the huge bird struggling on the ground, wing pierced by the quills, oozing blood. She wasn't sure how, but she'd use those weapons to damage the snake.

Now the crack seemed lighter, softer, less scary. Even though Bubba was in there.

"Oh my, the sun is coming." A full night of work had left her weary. She fought the urge to go to her nest, where she would normally be at this time. One more thing to do.

Clamping her teeth around the mirror—Grandma Mimi's gift—she dragged it closer to the crack. Although still cautious of the snake, she knew she was safe because she was cold. And the snake was a cold, coiled Bubba blob—but a big one—fast asleep. Later he would seek warmth from the sun.

He's like a big slug right now. Does a slug sleep or slurp? Her thoughts blurred as she moved the last piece of her plan into place. *Maybe a slug slurps. Bubba is slurping. No, that's not right.* Not only was she thinking strangely, but she also had no fear for what was to come.

Before she realized, she was looking up, up into the crack. A mass of crooked sticks poked out. The old packrat home. She jumped out of her muddled thoughts and focused on her task.

"I need to set this thing right." She braced the mirror upright against a small rock, its edge snug against the cliff face. It seemed brighter than ever and reflected the textures and colors of the sandstone and plants behind her, blooming into a soft glow.

"The sun. The sun is rising."

With her insides churning, she dashed back to where she had attached the net to the tree trunks. She crouched under a sagebrush but felt exposed in the growing light. Scrunching into its branches even more, she watched the crack and waited. And waited. Her eyes sank into a doze.

The ground shook, pitching Flora into the branches of the bush. Muffling a cry, she looked toward the crack. The bright sunlight glared on the cliff wall and sticks jutting out. But there was something other than sticks.

Stretched alongside the crack was a long, mottled cylinder. It stayed in one place, yet moved and rippled, narrowing into a perfectly formed tip that left the wall.

CHAPTER THIRTY-FOUR
BEWITCHING POWER

There he is. Beast of beasts. Evil one. Eater of packrats. Monster who took my ancestral home. She barely breathed. Did not dare move. The snake stretched along the base of the wall, no farther than a jangly-crate away. A rock hid his head from her view.

Oh, he's big. Longer than the woodpile. Fatter than me. How can he move with no feet? His head— it must be giant with pointy fangs and spikey horns and red eyes and smoke belching from his nostrils.

Flora shivered. As she stared at that hulking

body, she attached multiple heads and snarling jaws and bulging muscles. His power choked her with terror. *Stop it, Flora!* But she couldn't stop it. Until Paco's song crept into her head, melting her chilling vision and relaxing her.

I have a good plan. Maybe a few teensy-weensy holes in it...But everything is in place like I wanted. I pinned the net in those trees. Everything's perfect.

She looked, admiring her work. Then caught her breath. *Oh no, what is that, fluttering like a butterfly up there? Didn't I get all that stuff out of the net?* In the growing daylight, a long piece of whitish something dangled from the top of the net. That bright flag gave away the net's presence.

What is that? Flora cocked her head. She could almost see through its filmy whiteness. It looked like a flexible tube, patterned with dimples and grooves, crinkling and swaying.

Flora gulped. *It's a snakeskin, like what Grandma Mimi described. No wonder I wanted the crazy quilt to catch a snake. It's already caught one, or at least its skin.*

She tried to reason with her rising panic. *My plan can still work. He can't notice that skin. It can still work.*

The shadows had faded, lighting the snake. But his head was still hidden. A pattern of dark splotches ran the length of his body. Background colors of yellows and cream blended with the sand colors of the cliff.

He's gorgeous. His skin gleams like the skin of an eggplant, and his color is perfect camel...er, camouflage. I could mistake him for a big stick... Kind of like the owl, who seemed to melt into the night sky with its quiet feathers and big eyes.

Thoughts of the snake as a packrat killer drifted away. *He's not ugly. He's handsome and powerful.* As she stared and admired his perfection, the snake bewitched Flora, capturing her senses. But only for a moment.

His dark blotches moved, catching her breath.

She firmed her jaw. *I know what I must do. He has to leave our home.*

Flora smacked her mouth. From a rock next to the snake came a low, quivering tone that grew louder, until it erupted into a strange chant:

"Bubba bubba bubba boo,

Be-boppa boobie, bugaloo.

Bugga do dop, boppa bee,

boodle doobie bee bop,

boop bugga pee!"

A sleek sinewy head rose—slowly, elegantly, like a frond unfurling from the earth. It turned one direction, then twisted toward Flora.

No, no! He's not supposed to see me. That was my best ventriloquist voice. He's supposed to look at the talking rock!

But the snake faced Flora, crouched under the bush. A forked sliver spit out and in from his mouth, tasting the air. Dark streaks crossed his upper and lower jaws like big staples. The light-colored scales around his mouth gleamed. No puffing nostrils, no fangs, just a smooth head about the size of Flora's.

Oh my! He's looking right at me. Isn't he? Maybe not...He's still cold. He doesn't want to move yet. He mustn't move yet!

The head rose higher. And higher, halfway up the cliff, it seemed to Flora. His neck swayed a slinky dance. So graceful. His tongue slurped the air. So horrid. His head turned away from Flora, and his long body kept curling into graceful swirls.

From beyond the snake, where Flora had placed Grandma Mimi's gift, came another chant:

"Hello Bubba, you're not alone.

Be gone, big Bubba,

Vacation my home!"

Stupid, stupid, stupid! Vacation? Vacation? The word is vacate, Flora! And that voice was preposterous! Ridiculous. Preposterous. The snake jerked his head and faced the mirror. She stopped scold-

212

ing herself. *Aha, just what I wanted. And he's still cold and lazy.*

Flora's stomach nearly leaped from her insides. *What's happening? What's that noise? That's not part of the plan. His tail...*Shaking the ground, rattling loose leaves, his tail stirred the sandy dirt into a cloud. His body puffed and grew thicker as it slid and curled around itself. Then came monster breaths—bloodcurdling hisses from his wide-open mouth. She gulped, arched her back, and let out a low cry. But he was directing his actions toward the mirror. Not her.

My plan is working. He sees another snake in the mirror, but it's himself. Flora almost jumped with delight. But she had to be patient. *He needs to get good and confused.*

Hissing. Tail-shaking. The snake in the mirror stayed. Hissing. Tail-shaking. The snake in the mirror hissed and shook his tail back.

"Bubba wants to sleep in the sun," whispered Flora. "He never thought he'd meet another snake." She chuckled quietly. In fact, she chuckled too loudly. Hissing stopped. Tail-shaking stopped. The snake swung his head toward her.

Nostrils dipped; his head got bigger. His pronged tongue lapped the trails of her scent. He was coming right for her.

This was it. She knew what she must do.

Flora crept out from under the bush and offered her juicy packrat goddess body to the packrat-killing beast.

CHAPTER THIRTY-FIVE
FACING DEATH

His clear eyes glinted. His mouth opened a sliver. The air thickened, like a muddy pool of rotting plants and stinking fish.

He was supposed to be cold and lazy. But it seemed like an army of little feet on his underside all worked together, pushing him along in the sand.

Slicing through the mucky air, Flora bounced and thumped her hind leg and dashed back and forth, with only a net between them. She wanted to run, run far away.

But the moment of facing her foe, facing her death, held her fast. She kept hopping and pounding and hopping and pounding.

Until he went *around* the net, heading directly toward Flora. She skidded to a halt and backed up a few hops.

That's when the awful truth hit her. This snake was clever. Perhaps cleverer than she was.

Like a furry rock she stood, eyes wide, heart pounding, insides dropping. That tongue, oh that tongue. Dark and wicked it kept flicking. His eyes grew bigger and seemed to wrap around her head.

She would accept her fate.

Her short packrat life flashed in pictures, all mixed up with whiskers and cracks and sticks and shiny things. In an instant it passed, then something clicked. From deep inside Flora, tiny flags waved, and they grew into a big flag, red and stiff and making lots of noise. She couldn't stand there, staring at a snake who tasted her warm juiciness.

She moved. Perhaps not the best move. But she moved. She flexed her leg muscles, and *boing!* Off the ground, she leaped like a coiled spring. At the top of her *boing!*, when she was in that odd time of going neither up nor down, she looked down at the snake's head, the end of a thick squiggle.

On her way down she spun. Her front paws became her back paws, and her back paws became her front. Her head was where her tail had been when she first blasted off. *Plop!* Right next to the snake she landed then ran. Heart in her throat, she dashed to a jumble of boulders, plunged into a dark space, and squirmed and wriggled deep into a crack.

She was certain Bubba was behind, nostrils flaring, mouth open, ready to snag an ear, a paw, her tail. She thought she heard another hiss, spitting a chill on her wiggling bottom. *Faster, faster. Aha! A spot of light. Must get there. Faster!*

Her paws dug, spraying loose pebbles and sand. *Into his eyes. Blind him. Move, Flora!*

The spot of light! Right in front of her. That's what it was—a mere spot, where rocks met, an opening about the size of Flora's head.

Oh no. I can't get through there. I'm trapped. I'm doomed. She panted so loudly she couldn't hear him behind her. *Snakes are silent killers.* That was her last thought before she dove. Right into the spot of light. She had no choice. No turning around, no going back. Bubba was right there, under the rock, spitting on her tail.

But Flora dove into a problem. A big one. Her head went through the opening into the light, but most of her stayed on the other side, wriggling and scratching dirt, kicking sand at Bubba's face. Things felt kind of—snug. Her jiggly rolls plugged the opening, billowing out on both sides. Somehow, she pulled one paw through and kept kicking the others.

Oh no, oh no. Oh no no no! Is this my death? She squirmed; her skin stretched. She held her breath and blew her breath. She yelped and squealed. All those sublime eggplants. All those prickly pear pads, tender green shoots...she wished she'd never set eyes on food, the munch mound, all the treats...But she kept kicking and panting and squishing her insides until every bulge squeezed through that passage. The awful fright from a snake snapping at her rear unplugged her, like the time when Flora crammed too many berries from the berry patch in her mouth and she couldn't even chew but then she sneezed—blasting a frothy mess into the air.

Now Flora herself blasted into the light. She hit the ground running, and dashed to the top of the boulder, high above where she had plunged beneath it.

She checked her tail; it was still there. But where was her enemy? From her perch, she scanned the ground. Her net was in the trees. But no Bubba. No tracks. Had he disappeared?

He's still under the boulder, trying to turn around. Nope, she would have seen his tracks, wiping out the scatter of paw prints she left as she dashed that way.

Oh no, what if snakes can fly! She glanced above, just in case. No flying Bubba. It was too quiet. *He's planning a sneak attack. But I'm cleverer than he is. I'll find him. I'll flush him out.* Drawing a deep breath, she settled her voice way back in her throat, the way Dayana had taught her, and sent it right into the dark crack in the cliff. Her song boomed, shaking the thick morning air.

"Memories fixed in special marks
Brightening a space so dark.
Paws, whiskers, teeth, and ears
Mixed with joy and mamas' tears.

A sleek invader halts the light
Squeezes shining hearts so tight.
Gloom creeps in, fear does fall
Making packrat voices small, voices small.

'We laugh no more,' the voices cry
'Our spirits fade, our stories die.'
The chain of love knows no home
Forced to wander, forced to roam.

But young Flora stops and listens
To tales of old and yearnings risen.
A spark of hope, a gift to give
Stories swell, begging to live.

Dreams grow big, so very big.
Bubba. No more!"

Flora puffed her goddess body as a little smile crept over her face. No packrat killing snake was going to take over her family's special place, her family's story!

She sharpened her gaze and again scanned the ground below. Aha! Aha! Hidden in plain sight, looking like a bunch of leaves and sticks was Bubba, all knotted up right where she had landed after her *boing!* and spin.

Now it was time. Her destiny was swirling around her and she needed to grab it. She scampered down the boulder and dashed around him, to the other side of the net. Dancing again, she cried a wounded squeak, hoping to tempt him.

He raised his head and slithered toward the cliff, toward the net, toward Flora dancing on the other side. Oh, that big head with the slurping tongue searching, searching for her. His head rose. Higher. And higher. Above the net attached to the slender trees.

No, no, he can't go that high! He sees that white skin, he sees the net. Is that his skin? He knows the net is there. Such a stupid, stupid plan!

He slid up a tree and wound himself around its branches, bypassing her net fastened on the next tree. *It's true. Snakes can climb trees. And he's climbed the wrong one.*

How can those small branches hold such a big creature? The branches bent and the trunk swayed under his bulk. His head swung in the air and he gazed on Flora, panting below.

She groaned. *Now I've done it. He's in the wrong place, he's angry, and he's warming up before he attacks.*

But it's not over yet, Bubba. Heart throbbing in her throat, Flora dashed to the other side of the net, forcing the snake to turn his head around while his eyes followed her dance, back and forth, up and down.

Sssss!! Wide-open mouth. Sharp fangs. Pink tunnel. Baby packrats disappearing...

The snake pushed his head toward Flora, licking her fear, teasing her. Ready to strike. She backed up and skipped from side to side. He lowered his head, leaning toward her. The tree bent under his bulk. Icy barbs shot from his hard, yellow eyes.

SNAP!! Flora gasped. Loops of snake flew off the broken branch into a big saggy curve. He struggled to hoist himself back to a solid branch but instead caught his swinging body in the net below. Like a claw curling pincers around its prey, the net drew Bubba the snake into its grip.

The snake lost eye contact with Flora. While he hissed and thrashed, Flora removed the cactus spines that fastened the net to the trees. The loose net wrapped the snake ever more tightly.

His thick body dropped from the tree, pulling the net completely from its tree stakes. The snake writhed, winding himself in the cocoon trap. Folds of the net bound his head, pinning his jaws shut.

He lay still.

Flora grabbed the quill spears she had planted in the ground earlier and crept closer, peering into his eyes. She wondered at their clarity, their focus on her. Shaking her head, she detached from those eye hooks, and looked at her enemy.

"I did it. I did it. Bubba the snake is doomed. He can't escape my trap. He can't go back into our packrat home. He can't eat any more packrats. I've taken back our ancestral home!" She twirled and thumped her foot. Her whiskers danced circles.

"I'm going to finish him off right now with these quills. So easy! Right into those eyes!" Flora flinched. Had she really felt that thought, said those words?

The snake struggled, squirming and wiggling, but the net held him fast. He opened his mouth a slit and spat a throaty hiss, but he seemed too tired to make another sound.

Stillness crept over the scene, clearing away the gunky air from moments earlier. Flora coolly analyzed the situation.

"He thought he had me. He didn't think I could conquer him. But I did. Bubba snake deserves it." She wasn't sure exactly what the "it" was—being conquered by a packrat? Getting skewered in the eyes? Dying?

Bubba. She had called him that to make him seem less scary. So she could defeat him. But now he wasn't so scary. Naming him made him seem less like a monster and more like an animal. Like herself.

Flora decided she should not call him Bubba again. She thought about his death. "He's going to die right here, the snake's going to die, the snake's going to die." She raised a quill with her paw and pounded it to the ground every time she said "die." Over and over she said it, until she heard only the sounds of the words and the tapping of the quill while the meaning floated away.

Then she heard something else. A whisper— soft, but clear.

Help. Help.

Flora jumped and shook her head. Was that a voice in the air? In her head? Who was that? The head of the snake rested on the ground. He parted his upper and lower jaws as much as the bindings allowed. His tongue flicked out and in, out and in. Flora looked into those eyes with the round black pupils and knew the source of the voice.

*Like the owl...this snake is talking to me in my head...*Flora set her jaw and thought, *I don't want to listen to you, snake. I won't help you. You ate my family, you took over our home, and it's my destiny to...to...take back our old packrat home.* His patterned scales shivered in the tangled net. His tongue lashed. Out and in, out and in. The snake voice in her head persisted. *Help. Go. Go.* Out and in, out and in. Slices of pink flushed inside his mouth.

She wasn't sure snakes could talk. But Flora spoke aloud as she raised the quill and shook it. "Snake, I see your problem. But don't you understand? You were living in my packrat home and you ate Gertrude's and Grandma Mimi's babies.

You were going to eat me! You must die, don't you see? You must die!"

Flora pressed her mouth shut. She had never told a creature it must die. King Cyrus had demanded the owl die after it was wounded, but she argued for saving it. What was different now? Who was she to make a life or death decision for an animal? She had wanted to defeat this monster, but must he die from her actions?

By now she had lowered Paco's quill and was running her paw up and down the smooth shaft. She knew the tiny barbs at the end could do a lot of damage to a snake—especially his eyes. It would be so easy. One swift plunge.

One swift plunge.

And yet...She dropped the quill. She had to think.

Flora would decide if Bubba lived or died. A very gruesome death. A slow death. Having this power filled her with wonder. In fact, it frightened her.

The voice continued in her head. *Help. Help. Go. Rest. Cold time.*

The sun was melting the frost off the boulder surfaces. *Cold time is near. He must need to find a place to rest,* she thought.

Flora brooded. Bubba the snake, who could

climb trees and shed his skin and move with no feet reminded her of the owl. Both could move and hunt without drawing notice. They both blended into their surroundings—the owl flew silently, and the snake's colors made him melt into a backdrop of sticks and plants.

And they both ate packrats. Baby packrats even.

Yet the owl did not eat her. It wanted to eat her, but Paco's quills stopped it. And she saved its life by removing the quills. The owl helped her find her home. Possibly even saved her life.

Flora couldn't help calling the snake "Bubba" while she thought about him. She thought about his tail shaking, his mouth hissing, his retreat up the tree, his head swaying, his tongue tasting her: out and in, out and in. *Ready to kill me!*

His eyes softened; his tongue flicked. *Trouble, trouble.*

"Oh!" A thought hit her. "So—*you* were scared? Scared of the other snake you saw? Scared of *me*?"

Trouble, trouble.

Flora was certain. Bubba had felt he was in danger and was afraid for himself. Even though he could squeeze animals to death, he had enemies, too. *Same as the powerful owl. Paco's quills nearly killed him. Maybe I'm like Paco to this snake?*

The voice in her head grew louder. *Help. Go. Trouble. Trouble. Go.*

Flora sighed. She turned to the cliff. The old packrat home bulged with sticks. They pushed past the darkness in the crack, catching glints of sunshine. Breathing almost. She looked at the home, slipped into deep thought, slipped into that home. For a moment, she was a stick in that ancient place, joined with all the other sticks.

Her body was all abuzz. But after looking into that place, she knew what she needed to do. She would make one of the biggest decisions of her life. *We share this world. Maybe it's big enough for all of us. But Bubba and packrats need to stay away from each other.*

Turning to the snake she said, "Bubba snake, you will never ever go into our home again. I have the power to stop you, cause you pain. Even take your life. I will do this again if I have to. You must leave and go far away. Never return. Do you understand?" She stood big in her power. Big in her voice.

A wave of relief and gratitude from the beast bound in the net washed over Flora. She knew without a doubt that once freed, the snake would leave and not bother that place again.

Flora fetched the mirror. With its sharp edges,

she sliced and chopped the strong threads of the net. The tired snake lay quietly. Piece by piece the tangle fell away. A bit remained, covering his head and part of his body. He peered at Flora, flicking his tongue.

"I think I can cut this last bit off, Bubba, but you must not move. Then afterward you must leave." Her heart pounded. She would have to climb on top of that head with the teeth. And jaws. And tongue...His body was quiet for the other part of the net removal. But working around his head was different.

Go. Go. The snake voice was clear.

Working from the ground, Flora sliced strands behind the head, then stopped. *That's enough, Flora.*

"Go snake, go now." Flora hopped backward. The snake's body was free of the net, except for the small piece around his head. He would have to shake that bit off himself.

Flora held the mirror upright, bracing it between herself and the snake. With his snout and eyes still bound, he turned his head toward Flora and the mirror. His eyes widened and his head drew back. He saw another snake in the mirror and seemed to remember everything he just survived. He understood. This would be his place no longer.

Go. Trouble. Trouble. Rest.

Dipping his head, he glided toward the crack, zigzagging along. He paused below the crack, then moved on with stronger energy. As Flora watched Bubba disappear, she heard his voice in her head.

Brave animal. Big power.

#

Leaves rustled. A whiptail lizard scampered on a sunny rock. Flies buzzed. A stillness, full and safe, wrapped Flora, filling every strand of fur. When she looked to the crack, she could almost see clusters of whiskers twitching, hear their scampering, and sense their happiness from feeling safe again in their home.

A prickly pear cactus, small but tempting, drew Flora's hungry mouth. The pad burst with flavor as slobber oozed down her chin. "Utterly sublime!"

The bright morning light stabbed Flora's eyes. Normally she would be in her dark nest in the jangly-crate, sleeping peacefully. But everything was different now. She had gutted her nest of its treasures, and with Gertrude had dropped some of them nearby. Grabbing her favorites, she ran to the base of the crack, pausing at the spot where she had captured the snake.

Eagerly she entered that dark passage. She weaved through sticks, cactus spines, twigs, and animal droppings, all stuck together with many lifetimes of packrat urine. It smelled wonderful. She felt eager and welcome and big and alive.

When she reached the heart of the jumble, she placed her special treasures. "This is where these belong," she said as she laid five of Paco's quills. "They're for good luck." Then the treasure that had thrilled her packrat senses—the red doodad she had snatched from the two-legged pup's creation—went onto a perfect little ledge where it glowed like a firefly.

"The ancestral packrat home. I've added my special mark. And now it's *my* place, too." Flora beat her hind foot. She bounced like she was on a trampoline until she fell over and snuggled into that ancient place. Shreds of dried grass softened the darkest spot. "This must be where they slept," she mumbled.

A song threaded its way through the refuge. Not the soft lullaby that had calmed her racing thoughts in the past, but a new song. It grew and grew and burst into a fountain of colorful sparkles. Each sparkle became a voice. Each voice joined the others, and they sang together, those sparkle voices, in celebration. Flora filled with the song. Her fur and whiskers puffed and quivered, until she became a sparkle voice and sang too.

Flora felt her friends there, joining the celebration. Dayana the Fabulous laughed on her back. King Cyrus, with cheeks bulging, cried, "Well done!" Paco shook his mane of stickery quills and sang. Yellow saucer eyes blinked.

The dark empty spots in her heart filled with the light of her friends but also with the story of the great packrat birthplace, and of all the packrats that had ever lived there. A connection to her bigger packrat family had been missing, but now it was deep in her heart. She belonged to a bigger story. And sharing in that story, she left her special mark. Everything made perfect sense, including Grandma Mimi's words: *It is the place that makes us who we are.*

Grandma Mimi's gentle face, happy and glowing, appeared. She showered love on Flora. "You found your way, Flora. I am so proud of you!"

Flora's full heart spoke. "Everything is perfect." She nuzzled into that old packrat body and slept and slept.

CHAPTER THIRTY-SIX
GONE

"Flora, oh Flora, where are you?"

Flora's eyes fluttered open. A strange picture came into focus—bunches of cactus spines, twigs, shreds of juniper bark, seed hulls, pebbles. All placed by the paws of countless packrats before her. All mixed together in a web of amber-colored, hardened packrat cement.

This isn't my nest. Then she saw the red doo-dad and the porcupine quills she had placed, and thought, *everything is perfect, just as I like it.*

"Flora, please answer me!" A frightened voice pleaded in the distance.

Flora hopped to her senses.

"I'm here! I'm here, Gertrude!"

Flora crept through the maze to the edge of the packrat home, low in the crack, where she peered into the dusky evening, searching the bushes near the cliff.

"Gertrude, up here. In the crack, in the old packrat home."

A movement in the starlit shadows caught her eye.

"Flora, oh Flora. Are you alright? I'm so scared."

"I'm coming, Gertrude." She scampered down the crack to the ground and found Gertrude, shivering in a bush near where Flora had netted the snake.

The cousins sniffed each other's faces and danced, unable to hold back their joy.

"I found you, I can't believe I found you, Flora."

"Yes, but," Flora spluttered. "*Gertrude*, what are you—I told you—"

"I know—I know...b-but I was frightened—and—we—*I*—waited and waited. But then... oh, Flora, I didn't want to *lose* you!"

Flora looked fondly at Gertrude, who had said she would never go near the dreaded cliff again.

"Oh Gertrude, you are so brave. But everything is wonderful. The snake is gone. He won't return. I'm sure of it. And the best part is now we have our true home, our ancestral packrat home."

Flora's happy words made Gertrude smile, but only briefly. Gertrude knew nothing about the old packrat home. Or how the beast had eaten Grandma Mimi's babies and had driven her away. Flora explained its history to Gertrude.

A lonely tear slid down Gertrude's cheek.

"Don't cry, Gertrude, Grandma Mimi will be so happy, and now we're safe."

Gertrude's voice trembled. "That's just it, Flora. Grandma Mimi is...gone."

"Gone? What do you mean? She spoke to me, she's gotten stronger, and she's here...Isn't she?" Flora looked at her cousin as her heart felt a ripping pain. Gertrude's tears confirmed her fears.

"Oh, Flora. I stayed with her for a long time after you left us. She slept and slept. When she woke up, she was confused. She kept mumbling things like 'home, home, go home' and 'remember' and 'at last, at last.' I tried to walk her to her nest. But she dragged herself toward the dreaded cliff and climbed onto a rock and stared and stared. The last thing she said was 'home.' She looked so peaceful, and went to sleep, right there on the rock. I couldn't get her to budge." Gertrude was sobbing and could barely continue.

"I went to my nest because the sun was rising. I should never have left her."

Flora nuzzled her cousin and shared her tears.

"I looked all over for her this evening. I couldn't find her, Flora; she's gone. She's gone." Gertrude wept, Flora wept. For most of her life, wise old Grandma Mimi had longed to return to her home bearing the marks of her ancestors. Now she could never experience what would have been her greatest joy.

At that moment Flora's heart was slashed wide open.

CHAPTER THIRTY-SEVEN
MIRROR IMAGE

Shadows deepened and stars brightened. A crisp breeze fanned the cottonwood trees near the cliff, shuffling their drying leaves. Some lost their grip and surrendered to random puffs that made them twirl and bounce and chatter with each other.

The cousin packrats watched the leaves dance around them. They sniffed the decay of moist plants mounded near the cliff wall—a foreign scent because they had always avoided the dreaded cliff.

Together they moved to a clump of prickly pear pads where they gnawed, trying to fill the emptiness in their hearts.

Flora sighed, letting her eyes drift. A flash nearby—a sparkly wrinkle—attracted her. Gertrude joined her as they crept to the smooth treasure. Grandma Mimi's gift was propped upright near the rocks and tree trunks where Flora and the snake had clashed.

They crouched in front of the silky slick mirror.

"Oh my, look at us, Gertrude. Look at our reflection. Look at who we are."

Two magical creatures in the mirror—solid and strong, brimming with life—returned their gaze through dark, intelligent eyes.

As Flora peered more closely, she saw something else. Above their heads, in the reflection of the mirror, she saw the cliff with the darkest of cracks. Pinpricks of light glowed in that crack, shining like stars. They sprouted ears and whiskers that wiggled and danced. The brightest light grew and grew. Into an image. A smiling, ancient packrat. *You remembered, Flora. You remembered*! Oh, Grandma! Flora's heart swelled, at once sad and happy, and spilled over with love.

Flora turned with Gertrude and faced the deep

crack in the no longer dreaded cliff. Yes, she *did* remember. She remembered herself. Flora. She remembered a special, quiet place deep inside herself and she learned to go there and listen. She would forever know that place and trust it. Because that place helped her discover things about herself and the world she had never imagined.

She looked at the great packrat birthplace with the memories of her ancestors.

"I'm home," Flora said. "*We* are finally home!"

Animals in *The Dreaded Cliff*

While the animal characters in *The Dreaded Cliff* are fictional, they represent real animals in the American Southwest. Other than talking, singing, ventriloquism, ruling kingdoms and the like, the characters display authentic animal traits.

White-Throated Woodrat

Packrat, woodrat, trade rat—these are all common names for the rodent that collects shiny objects and builds a complex den that protects it from predators and temperature extremes. Its home includes tunnels, nesting chamber, food storage areas, and a "midden" of cast-off materials and packrat poop. Packrats use dens tucked in rock crevices for thousands of years, covering the midden with urine that crystalizes. These time capsules preserve scraps that help scientists understand changes in the area's climate, plants, and animals. Solitary and active year-round, a packrat sometimes shares its den in wintertime with a snake during its restful, "torpor" time.

Ord's Kangaroo Rat

It's not a rat or a kanga-roo, but the huge hind feet of the kangaroo rat can propel it from six to nine feet in a single bound. Adapted well to hot dry conditions, it retreats to its underground burrow during the day, plugging the entry holes to maintain a stable temperature and humidity. Sleeping with its nose buried in its fur creates a pocket of moist air. It carries its nighttime collections of food in fur-lined pouches on the outside of its cheeks, and stores seeds in its burrow or in shallow pits called "caches." Although a kangaroo rat drinks water when available, it processes water from its diet of dry seeds, providing all that it needs.

North American Porcupine

Among the coarse hairs of the porcupine are about 30,000 special hairs—stiff quills with tiny backward-facing barbs at the tips that anchor them in the flesh of an attacker. When threatened, a porcupine erects its quills, making it appear bigger and skunk-like with black and white markings. It stamps its feet, clatters its teeth, and shivers its body for further warning. Next, it emits a strong odor from a spot above its tail. If it attacks, it runs backward or swings its tail into the predator, planting its quills. Although its long claws make it a skillful tree climber, sometimes a porcupine falls and sticks itself—but antibiotic qualities of its quills help prevent infection.

Desert Cottontail Rabbit

Almost any animal that a cottontail rabbit can't outrun will snack on it, but certain traits and behaviors help it survive. Its large eyes located on the sides of its head see well in the dark and to the side, front, and back—all at the same time. It limits food hunting to early morning and late evening, and rarely goes out in windy conditions when it can't hear a predator's approach. If it senses danger, it freezes in place, then dashes off in a zig-zag pattern as fast as 18 miles per hour.

Most cottontail rabbits live no more than one to two years. A mother rabbit can produce up to 25 babies, or kits, in one breeding season, helping to maintain the population.

American Badger

With its broad flat body, stubby legs, and heavy clawed feet, the badger is a dirt-moving machine. It can dig faster than any ground dwelling rodent—a useful skill when pursuing a meal of a ground squirrel, pocket gopher, kangaroo rat, or prairie dog into the animal's burrow. Usually solitary, a badger sometimes hunts alongside a coyote. The coyote waits to snatch an animal leaving its burrow as the badger digs. Likewise, the badger waits for a rodent headed for its burrow as it escapes a coyote. When cornered, a badger might hiss and fake an attack, use its sharp teeth and strong claws on the attacker, or burrow quickly out of sight. It can run backwards as fast as it can run forward.

Great Horned Owl

Built for hunting, especially at night, the great horned owl ambushes prey from high perches. Its large cylinder-shaped eyes give superb night vision and act like telephoto lens  es. Although its eyes are anchored in their sockets, the owl can twist its head 270 degrees to look in nearly any direction. The disc-shaped face directs noises to ears located at different levels on its head, which help it pinpoint an animal's location. Ragged feather edges muffle the sound of the owl flying. Powerful talons easily crush the skulls of rabbits, packrats, skunks, and other heavy prey, which it can carry away, despite weighing over three times more than itself. The feathered "ear" tufts have nothing to do with hearing or hunting—but may give territorial messages to other owls.

Great Basin Gopher Snake

Also called a bullsnake, the gopher snake is a good climber, swimmer, and burrower. It has a thin, flexible flap or "epiglottis" in its trachea that vibrates when a stream of air passes over it, producing a loud hissing. When defending itself, in addition to hissing, the gopher snake puffs and elevates its body, flattens its head into a triangle, and shakes its tail, mimicking a rattlesnake. It is non-venomous, and instead constricts its prey with body coils or presses an animal against its burrow wall to subdue it before swallowing it whole. It can constrict three nestling birds or rodents in separate body coils at the same time, preventing their escape.

Acknowledgments

This story grew over many years and many people assisted and inspired me along the way.

Special thanks to Uma Krishnaswami, children's author and friend, whose writing workshop I attended years ago when my story was first coming to life. Her valuable critique and guidance at that time encouraged me to keep going. Uma's continued teachings, creativity, insights, and contributions in children's literature have inspired me deeply.

I am indebted to Geoff Habiger of Kinkajou Press for taking a chance with me and my debut novel. His skillful editing and comments strengthened the authenticity of Flora's voice and improved the final chapters. I am thankful he championed the inclusion of illustrations and offered spot-on suggestions for their final appearance. Thanks to illustrator Odessa Sawyer for her amazing work and for responding with good humor and skill to my suggestions.

Thanks to Traci HalesVass and students in her San Juan College creative writing class, who read chapters and provided valuable comments that improved my writing. Many thanks to those in my writing critique group who read my manuscript and provided helpful suggestions: Vicky Ramakka, whose editorial eye is unmatched, Linda Fredericks, who suggested chapter headings and laughed at all the right places, and Thelma Daly, who gave comments and encouragement. I am grateful to Rhenna St. Clair, who read the manuscript and offered comments that helped me deepen the characters and fill in missing pieces. Thanks to those in the Persistence Club and Writers Drink Coffee group, especially Vicki Holmsten, who provided great fellowship and practical suggestions as I searched for ways to bring my story to the world. Friends Trudi Pierce, Kristie Arrington, Chris Moon, and Lydia Velose all kept me sane along the way, distracting me or encouraging me when I needed it.

Special thanks to my son Dylan Simmons who listened to repeated readings of passages and made sage comments as only he can do. Thanks especially to Richard Simmons who freely offered his impressions and encouragement.

Fond thanks to Dayana of Copan Ruinas, Honduras, and Jacob Adler, who inspired me to remember my child's voice as my characters came to life.

Author's Note

Packrats share my home in northwestern New Mexico, where they bring me delight but sometimes cause great displeasure. They nibble my eggplants in planter boxes, leaving poop and sticky urine on the deck. They drag eggshells, onion skins, and melon rinds from the compost pile, scattering trails of food scraps beneath juniper trees and into the garage. A packrat wiped out my tomato seedlings one night, despite the protective netting and generous dusting of cayenne pepper I left around the plants. I made peace with him, though, by leaving vegetable scraps every few nights, diverting him from his love of spicy seasonings on tender new plants.

My vehicles are a favorite packrat hangout. They love decorating under the hood, where they leave cactus spines, juniper berries, and loads of sticks—whatever makes them comfy. I've suffered embarrassment at car lube shops, where the mechanic has warned me to check more often under the hood as he picked out the trash left by a packrat. Once a mechanic and I discussed the senseless (and expensive) vandalism a hoodlum had committed on my vehicle's horn wires before I later realized the culprit was a packrat.

Those are some of the bothersome packrats. But then there was the packrat that had built its nest on the protective metal shield beneath the '79 Volkswagen van floorboard. That brave packrat traveled with my husband and me across southern Utah. When we tried to sleep at night, she made a racket as she deposited objects she had collected for her nest. But by morning she had settled down in her refuge, anxious to continue her great adventure to the next camping spot.

I had seen plenty of packrat middens tucked in the cracks of cliff walls in this region. And I started thinking about our stowaway packrat, traveling to the unknown, going about her packrat life along the way. But what if that packrat got separated from her nest, and what if there was a midden, crammed with packrat memories...and predators, friends, hope, yearnings, a reluctant hero, and Southwest canyons and creatures? It was a story that kept nagging me until I allowed it to emerge in *The Dreaded Cliff*.

About the Author

Terry Nichols is a retired National Park Service ranger who left her childhood home in Cincinnati, Ohio to work in parks in the high desert and canyon country of the Southwest. She traded her ranger life of writing trail guides, interpretive brochures, articles, teacher guides, professional papers, and bureaucratic reports for a journey of writing for children. Terry is fond of wandering and has published over 100 blogs about her travel experiences. Mother of two grown sons, she lives in Aztec, New Mexico, where she writes and talks to packrats and lizards every chance she gets.

You can learn more at Terry's website: terryfnichols.com